𝔉oreign 𝔆lassics for 𝔈nglish 𝔅eaders

EDITED BY

MRS OLIPHANT

SCHILLER

The Volumes published of this Series contain—

DANTE, ... By the EDITOR.

VOLTAIRE, By Major-General Sir E. B. HAMLEY, K.C.M.G.

PASCAL, ... By Principal TULLOCH.

PETRARCH, ... By HENRY REEVE, C.B.

GOETHE, ... By A. HAYWARD, Q.C.

MOLIÈRE, . . . By Mrs OLIPHANT and F. TARVER, M.A.

MONTAIGNE, . . . By Rev. W. LUCAS COLLINS, M.A.

RABELAIS, ... By WALTER BESANT.

CALDERON, ... By E. J. HASELL.

SAINT SIMON, . . . By CLIFTON W. COLLINS, M.A.

CERVANTES, ... By the EDITOR.

CORNEILLE AND RACINE, . . By HENRY M. TROLLOPE.

MADAME DE SÉVIGNÉ, . . . By Miss THACKERAY.

LA FONTAINE, AND OTHER } By Rev. W. LUCAS COLLINS, M.A.
    FRENCH FABULISTS, }

SCHILLER, ... By JAMES SIME, M.A.

In preparation—

TASSO, ... By E. J. HASELL.

ROUSSEAU, ... By HENRY GRAHAM.

SCHILLER

BY

JAMES SIME, M.A.

AUTHOR OF 'LESSING : HIS LIFE AND WRITINGS '

WILDSIDE PRESS

CONTENTS.

CHAP.   PAGE

I. INTRODUCTION, ...   1

II. AT HOME AND AT THE MILITARY ACADEMY,   7

III. IN STUTTGART, ...   28

IV. IN MANNHEIM, ...   38

V. SCHILLER'S EARLY WRITINGS, . . .   54

VI. IN DRESDEN AND WEIMAR, . . .   68

VII. "DON CARLOS," AND SOME LYRICS, . .   86

VIII. IN JENA, ...   95

IX. SCHILLER'S PROSE WRITINGS, . . .   112

X. SCHILLER AND GOETHE, ...   127

XI. "WALLENSTEIN,"   158

XII. IN WEIMAR, ...   171

XIII. SCHILLER'S LAST DRAMAS, . . .   184

XIV. THE END, ...   210

SCHILLER.

CHAPTER I.

INTRODUCTION.

In his splendid Epilogue to "The Song of the Bell," written soon after Schiller's death, Goethe says of his friend that, in his mature years, "that which fetters us all—the common—lay far behind him." It would be impossible to indicate more exactly the quality which must impress every student of Schiller's career. Even in his appearance there was an aspect of greatness as he walked through the streets with his firm military step, his tall form towering above the passers-by. "His carriage, his walk, every one of his movements," said Goethe to Eckermann, "was proud and grand; but his eyes were mild." No one could talk with him without perceiving the loftiness of his aims; and always he felt, even to his last hours, that, whatever task he had accomplished, still wider worlds remained for him to conquer. For many years his life was one of almost con-

stant suffering; but pain could not break his iron will,
or turn him from the path on which he had elected to
march. The meanest subjects he strove to see in the
light of great ideas; and in his search for truth he never
allowed his judgments to become hard doctrines, but submitted them willingly to new tests, holding that man rises
to genuine dignity, not so much by what he believes as by
the temper in which he believes it. Schiller's poetry is
marked by the same grandeur of tone as that which characterised his thought and feeling. The passions which
he prefers to represent are high, enduring, and strenu-
ous—passions which, if gratified, create around them a
new world; which, if baffled, rend human nature in its
depths. With how many heroic forms has he not enriched modern literature!—forms which breathe the
spirit of his own inmost life, and which possess an
eternal freshness and vitality. Only the highest poets
of all—and Schiller does not rank with them—have the
capacity of appreciating equally the tragedy and the
comedy of existence. To humour he was not inaccessible,
but wit, in its most refined forms, was beyond his range;
and it was more natural to him to grasp his materials
boldly and firmly, than to handle them with a light
and delicate touch. The peculiarities of his genius
were not, however, incompatible with a fine feeling for
the gentler aspects of life; and amid the "crashing
splendours" of his heroic conflicts we often detect a
note of exquisite tenderness and pathos.

It is commonly said of Schiller, that in all his writing he is the representative and the advocate of a particular set of ideas. "Schiller," says Heine, "wrote for
the great ideas of the Revolution; he destroyed the

Bastille of the intellect, he aided in building the temple
of freedom." He had, it is true, a strong passion for
ordered liberty, and with this he combined an equally
strong sentiment of humanity. It was impossible for
him to refrain from expressing these elements of his
character in his works, and it is because he expressed
them that his highest conceptions convey so powerful an
impression of sincerity and truth. Moreover, his writings were one of the mightiest influences in arousing in
the German mind a longing for a worthier national life ;
and they still feed the flame which they helped to kindle.
It is, however, to do Schiller extreme injustice to suppose that he was nothing more than a proclaimer of new
social and political doctrines. Even in his earliest
dramas, which were the passionate utterance of long-sup-
pressed emotions, he did not altogether disregard the
claims of art ; and in his mature labours these claims became absolutely supreme. It was one of his fundamental
principles that the artist is not directly concerned with
the practical effect of his work ; that he has to think
only of its artistic quality. That a work of art, if its
artistic quality be true, will indirectly stimulate man's
moral nature by making him vividly conscious of his
power and freedom, Schiller firmly maintained ; but he
also maintained that to make this the end of art is to
conflict with its essential tendencies and to defeat its
proper aim. Hence when, in some of his chief dramas,
he introduces the conceptions of humanity and freedom,
he does so because through them, with his special temperament, he is able most directly and most powerfully
to achieve the purpose of tragedy ; and he determines
the character of their expression in accordance with the

artistic necessities of his scheme. It is, therefore, as an
artist, not as a prophet, that Schiller must be estimated ;
and it may be safely said that his art in its highest
manifestations, and within its own limits, is nearer perfection than that of any other master, Goethe alone ex-
cepted, in the literature of Germany.

The pessimistic philosophers, whose voices are so
potent in the Germany of to-day, indulge sometimes
in a quiet sneer at Schiller; but it would be an error
to represent him as indifferent to the facts on one
interpretation of which the pessimistic philosophy is
built up. Who, indeed, can be indifferent to them?
They thrust themselves before us too persistently to
be overlooked by the dullest and the most self-satis-
fied minds. And if the burden of the "world-pain"
rests at times on men of ordinary aptitudes, a man
of poetic genius, with more delicate susceptibilities, is
not likely to escape its pressure. Schiller, certainly,
did not escape it; and in several of his tragedies he
presents pictures as striking as any that have been
drawn in modern times of the working of those awful
powers which play with human happiness for ends we
cannot fathom. But Schiller, unlike the pessimists, did
not consider that the whole duty of man is to reflect on
his own misery. He recognised in the human spirit a
power to rise above the sorrows and struggles of time,
and to create for itself an ideal world in which the dis-
cords of reality are harmonised and its tempests stilled.
And he not only took refuge from the occasional meanness and pettiness of life in this larger sphere, but held
fast by the faith that the ideal world need not always
be a mere ideal, but that the course of history slowly

tends to give it form and body. Such ideals as his, we are told, are illusions; but they have their root in the ultimate ground of man's nature,—and may it not be that they are nearer the essential truth of things than the world which is called real? So Schiller reasoned; and his hope inspired him with courage, energy, and calm. In nearly all his mature works we feel the presence of this prevailing mood. He did not write to give it expression; but it created the atmosphere in which the figures of his imagination suffered or rejoiced, conquered or died.

The controversy as to the relative position of Schiller and Goethe in literature was long ago finally closed; but by undisputed right Schiller stands next to Goethe in the love and reverence of Germany. He, more than any other poet, has embodied in abiding forms what are believed to be the vital qualities of the German nature; and his countrymen delight to think of him, with his unresting vigour, his high aspirations, his sustained enthusiasm, as the ideal type of the national character. These claims need not be disputed; but Schiller, like Goethe, is too great to be merely the poet of a single nation. He has the true cosmopolitan touch, and his art gives him the pass-word that admits him to the company of the immortals.

Of the numerous biographies of Schiller, one of the earliest was Carlyle's; and, although necessarily written with inadequate materials, it has too much genius ever to be wholly superseded. More than twenty years after Schiller's death, his sister-in-law, Caroline von Wolzogen, herself endowed with poetic feeling, wrote a charming little biography, in which appeared for the first time many of his most interesting letters. There are also biographies by Hoffmeister (who wrote two books on Schiller, one of which has lately been made the basis of an elaborate work by Viehoff, Goethe's biographer), by Palleske (whose work has been translated into English by Lady Wallace), by Schwab, Boas, Goedeke, and others. A volume by Heinrich Düntzer, issued in 1881, brings together the facts of Schiller's life in strictly chronological order, and the narrative is illustrated by a number of excellent engravings. In addition to these works there are many volumes of Schiller's correspondence.

7

CHAPTER II.

AT HOME AND AT THE MILITARY ACADEMY.

JOHANN CHRISTOPH FRIEDRICH SCHILLER was born in
Marbach, in Würtemberg, on the 10th or the 11th (probably the 10th) November 1759. He came of a respectable Swabian stock, his grandfather and great-
grandfather having been prosperous bakers in Bittenfeld,
a village at the point where the Rems flows into the
Neckar. They were probably descended from Jacob
George Schiller, who was born in Grossheppach, another
Swabian village, in 1587; and they may have been
connected with Jörg Schiller, who in the early part of
the fifteenth century was famous as a Master Singer in
South Germany.

At the time of Schiller's birth, his father, Johann
Kaspar Schiller, was about thirty-six years of age, and
his life had been full of stir and excitement. After the
war of the Austrian succession, during which he was a
surgeon in a Bavarian regiment of hussars, he went in
the spring of 1749, " on his own horse," to visit a married sister in Marbach, a pretty little town on a vine-
covered hill overlooking the Neckar. He put up at
the " Golden Lion," and six months afterwards mar-

ried his landlord's pretty daughter, Elisabeth Dorothea
Kodweiss, who was then only seventeen. Before his
marriage he passed the State examination which em-
powered him to practise as a surgeon, and a little later
he acquired the right of citizenship in Marbach. As,
however, a village practice afforded small scope for his
energies, he soon began to think of resuming his old
life; and in 1753 he joined the army of his native
prince, the Duke of Würtemberg. He began with a
humble post, but was soon made an officer, and gradually rose to the rank of captain. He saw a good deal
of active service during the Seven Years' War, in which
the Duke of Würtemberg joined the Allies against the
King of Prussia. At the battle of Leuthen his horse
was shot under him; and he almost lost his life in a
morass during the flight of the Austrian left wing, to
which the Würtemberg troops were attached.

Meanwhile his young wife remained contentedly at
Marbach with her parents, who had fallen on evil times;
her father gradually sinking, through his own impru-
dence, from comparative wealth to poverty, until at last
he was glad to become keeper of one of the town gates.
Eight years after her marriage a new interest was added
to her life by the birth of her eldest daughter, Christophine; and two years later came Schiller. Four other
daughters were born, two only of whom survived infancy,
Louise and Nanette. The two latter were so much
younger than Schiller, that they exercised little direct
influence over him; but his eldest sister was his constant companion and friend. Her greatest pleasure was
to be permitted to share his amusements, and if he com-
mitted any little fault she would try to shield him from

punishment by pretending that she was chiefly to blame. All through life Schiller found in the affection and sympathy of this sister a source of strength and consolation.

Towards the close of the Seven Years' War Captain Schiller was stationed with his regiment in Ludwigsburg, where he was joined by his wife and their two children. In 1763, about Christmas, he was sent as a recruiting officer to the imperial city Schwäbisch-Gmünd, with permission to reside in the neighbouring village, Lorch; and thither he was followed in a few months by his family, from whom he was not again separated. Schiller, who had now entered his fifth year, was thus brought under the influence of both his parents. His father, as his career testifies, was a man of great vigour and independence of character; there was a look of keen intelligence in his dark, piercing eyes; and his whole bearing was that of a man who had fought his way successfully through life, and who knew his own worth. In manner he was so rigid that his children rather respected than loved him, yet they knew that beneath the rugged surface of his nature there were depths of true gentleness. The effect of his severe, sometimes harsh discipline, was softened by his refined and tender-hearted wife. She was tall, lithe, and graceful, with light-blue, rather weak, eyes, reddish hair, and a broad open forehead. Without being beautiful, her features were made interesting by the sweetness and dignity of their expression. Although an excellent "Hausfrau," she did not allow herself to be entirely absorbed by her domestic duties; she was fond of poetry, especially poetry of a religious tendency, and took pains to make it attractive to her children.

Lorch is a charming village on the eastern border of Würtemberg, from which may be seen, to the east, the ridges of the Rauhe Alp, and to the west the dim outlines of the Black Forest. Close at hand are various hills, past which, with their vines and pine-woods, flows the Rems, through fruitful valleys, to the Neckar. One of these hills is crowned by the ruins of a cloister, which was the burying-place of the Hohenstaufen family; and further off is the Hohenstaufen hill itself, on whose steep summit formerly stood the castle of this mighty race. In Lorch the family lived for three years, and Schiller always looked back upon them as among the happiest years of his life. He was a delicate child, with his mother's face and figure; of gentle manners, but bright, active, and intelligent. After his death his sister recalled with enthusiasm the pleasure with which he would abandon play to hear his father read, and the beauty of his expression as he knelt with folded hands at morning and evening prayers. He loved to roam with his sister through the ruined cloister; and sometimes their father would join them, and talk to them about the Hohenstaufen emperors, bringing in occasional touches from his own military experience.

Schiller received his first lessons in Latin from Pastor Moser, the chief clergyman of Lorch, who taught him along with his own son. Pastor Moser made a strong impression on Schiller, who afterwards gave his name to the clergyman in "The Robbers." Under the influence of this austere but not unkind teacher, he fancied that there was no life so glorious as that of a pastor; and at home, with a black gown thrown over his shoulders, he would sometimes mount upon a chair and deliver little

sermons, with his admiring mother and sister for a con-
gregation. The recollections of his childhood are not
all, however, of so serious a character, for we are told
that beautiful weather tempted him occasionally to prefer
the hills and meadows to the schoolroom. His mother
condoned these small offences, but carefully kept them
from his father's knowledge.

However happy Schiller may have been at Lorch, his
father was wretched; he hated the work of a recruiting
officer, and—such was the impoverished condition of the
Würtemberg treasury—he could not obtain a florin of
his pay. The birth of his second daughter, Louise, made
it absolutely necessary for him to improve his circumstances; and after various urgent applications he was
allowed, in the closing days of 1766, to rejoin his regiment in Ludwigsburg, where his arrears were gradually
made good. Frau Schiller was especially pleased by this
change, for Marbach is not very far from Ludwigsburg,
so that she was able to visit her aged parents sometimes.
On an Easter Monday, when walking over the hills on
this pious errand with her son and daughter, she talked
to them with so much feeling of Christ's journey with
the two disciples to Emmaus, that (according to Christophine) the children were deeply touched, and at last
burst into tears.

At this time Ludwigsburg was one of the most animated towns in South Germany; and it owed its temporary importance to the wilfulness of Duke Karl Eugen,
one of the petty despots who had so long been playing
with the destinies of the German people. Not wholly
without good impulses, he was in the main selfish, arbitrary, and tyrannical. A poll-tax having been lately im-

posed without the sanction of the States, a deputation from Tübingen waited upon him to represent the grievances of the Fatherland. " What Fatherland ? " cried the Duke, in feeble imitation of Louis XIV.; " I am the Fatherland." As Stuttgart also resented his tyranny, he marked his displeasure by transferring his residence from the capital to Ludwigsburg. Here he had a splendid palace and park ; and he rapidly built a large theatre, for which, at immense cost, he obtained singers and opera-dancers from Italy and France.

While in Ludwigsburg, the Schillers occupied a part of the house connected with the printing establishment of Cotta, who was afterwards Schiller's publisher. In the same house lived a brother officer, Von Hoven, in whose son, a lively, intelligent boy, Schiller found a pleasant companion. Behind the house Captain Schiller had a large garden, in which he devoted much of his time to the planting and nurture of trees. Botany and agriculture had interested him for many years, and, in 1767-69, Cotta published for him a work in four parts, entitled " Observations concerning Agricultural Matters in the Duchy of Würtemberg, by an Officer of the Duchy."

Although Schiller had only entered his eighth year when the family settled in their new home, he was too sensitive not to be impressed by the change from a remote village to the busy streets of Ludwigsburg, along which gaily dressed courtiers, and soldiers in bright uniforms, were constantly passing. Officers and their families were admitted free to the theatre ; and although Captain Schiller had no love for amusements of this kind, he was obliged to take occasional ad-

vantage of the privilege of his class. His son was
of course fascinated by the gorgeous spectacles in which
the Duke delighted; and now, instead of edifying his
mother and sister with sermons, he entertained them with
mimic tragedies, in which important parts were sustained
by figures cut out in paper. It was, however, the intention of his parents to devote him to the Church, and
he was accordingly sent to the Latin school of Ludwigsburg, which he attended for six years. In this school
there were three classes, each of which had a "precep-
tor" of its own — the third and second classes giving
almost their whole time to Latin, while in the first class
Greek and Hebrew were also taught. Pupils destined
for the pastorate were obliged to undergo periodical
examinations at Stuttgart, conducted for the Consistory
there by the rector of the Stuttgart Gymnasium. Schiller
went to his first examination at Easter, in 1769, and the
examiner reported that he was "a hopeful boy." After
the examination of 1771 he was again reported to be
"a hopeful boy," and it was added that he "had advanced not unsuccessfully on the path of letters." He
excelled in Latin verse; and his father, looking back
twenty years afterwards, recalled with pride his innumerable "disticha, carmina, epistolæ, &c."

In early boyhood Schiller was as distinguished in play
as in work; but in his thirteenth year he seems to have
become melancholy and thoughtful. For hours he would
walk about with a friend, pouring forth "complaints
against destiny," and talking much about "the mysterious future," and about "plans for his mature life." The
change had considerable effect on his work, for in 1772
his examiner reported that, although in the preceding

year his studies "had not been without fruit," he was
not quite equal to the pupils who had been examined
before him. In this same year he was confirmed, and
his mother, seeing him loitering in the street on the
evening before the ceremony, expostulated with him on
his indifference. Schiller silently retired to his room,
from which he emerged an hour or two afterwards with
a poem that is said to have astonished his parents by
the ardour of its religious feeling.

Having in 1772 almost completed his course at Ludwigsburg, Schiller was about to be sent to one of the
cloister colleges which formed a link between the Latin
schools and the theological "faculty" at the universities,
when all his plans and those of his parents were suddenly changed. At a beautiful country residence near
Stuttgart, called the Solitude, the Duke of Würtemberg
had established a school for the training of builders and
gardeners. By-and-by he transformed it into a school
for the education of officers; and now he was busily
engaged in extending it, so that it might provide a
supply of thoroughly cultivated officials for all branches
of the public service. Early in 1773 the school was established on its new basis, and received the name of "The
Military Academy." Meanwhile the Duke, who henceforth
devoted much attention to the Academy, had been seek-
ing for pupils; and he entered into communication with
Captain Schiller about his son. Both parents were sincerely anxious that Schiller should become a clergyman;
and this was his own earnest wish. The Duke's offers
were therefore politely declined; but, having made up
his mind that Schiller was the kind of pupil he wanted,
he expressed his desire in such terms that a second

refusal was impossible, and the elder Schiller even felt obliged to accede to his will with assurances of ardent gratitude for his princely beneficence. The agreement was that Schiller should remain in the Academy until the completion of the studies prescribed for him, when the Duke engaged to grant him an appointment suitable to his talents and aspirations. Subsequently, Captain Schiller gave a written promise that his son (who had not been consulted) would not, without the Duke's consent, abandon the career to which he might be summoned.

In accordance with this understanding, Schiller was entered by his father at the Military Academy on the 16th of January 1773. He was then thirteen years of age, and he did not leave the Academy until he was twenty-one. Of these eight years, which were as important as any period of his life, he spent about three at the Solitude and five in Stuttgart, whither the institution was transferred in November 1775, partly as a token of the heartiness of the Duke's reconciliation with his capital.

There were about three hundred pupils at the Academy, and they were divided into two sections, gentle and simple, or, as they were called, Chevaliers and Élèves. The Chevaliers dined by themselves at a horse-shoe table at the upper end of the dining-hall; their bedrooms were superior to those of the Élèves; and those of them who gained prizes were allowed to kiss the hand of the Duke, while the Élèves were obliged to content themselves (unless they gave proof of extra-ordinary ability and diligence) with kissing the hem of his coat. The life of all the pupils was as rigidly ordered as that of soldiers in barracks. They wore a special uniform; and if they violated in the slightest particular any of the numerous and minute rules, they exposed themselves to a variety of severe penalties. They slept in large rooms, about fifty in each; and in each room were stationed an officer and four inspectors. Punctually at five o'clock in summer, at six in winter, they rose, said prayers, dressed, and laid out their bed-clothes; they then marched to breakfast; and at seven o'clock the work of the day began. Classes continued until eleven, when they marched back to their bedrooms, made their beds, and put on their uniforms. Next they were carefully inspected, frequently by the Duke himself, who did not hesitate to strike with his cane any unfortunate youth whose hair had not been curled with sufficient stiffness, or who had neglected to polish his buckles. After dinner, which was at twelve, they were allowed to walk or to amuse themselves in the garden, where a piece of ground was set apart for each to cultivate as he might think best. From two to seven work was resumed; and at nine, after a light supper, all were in bed, with orders to maintain absolute silence.

The boys looked forward with some pleasure to Sunday, when, after attendance at church, they were allowed rather more freedom than usual in their walks in the neighbourhood, which commands splendid views of a fertile country dotted over with villages. On Sunday, too, they might be visited by their relatives, although grown-up sisters were rigidly excluded. Holidays were unknown; but all holy days were celebrated in much the same fashion as Sunday. The great day of the year was the 14th of December, the anniversary of the foundation of the institution. A fortnight before this date was devoted to examinations; and on the gala-day itself prizes were distributed by the Duke, amid much pomp and circumstance.

The professors were as a rule thoroughly efficient, the Duke being sensible enough to prefer young men of energy and enthusiasm, some of them only a few years older than their pupils. As order was maintained not by them but by inspectors, it was easier for them than for most professors to gain the confidence and love of their students, who would often consult them on matters that are generally carefully concealed from teachers. The isolation of the young men, and the strict discipline to which they were subjected, had at least one good effect,—it caused them to form warm friendships, which in many cases lasted throughout life. Individuality was crushed out of weak natures; but boys of powerful intellect cherished an ideal world of their own, all the more ardently because of the narrowness and rigidity of their ordinary routine. On the whole, with all its defects, the Academy must be said to have done much more good than harm. It is impossible not to respect an institution which, within a brief period, gave Schiller to literature, Dannecker to art, and Cuvier to science.

In his first year Schiller continued his general studies, adding to Greek and Latin, French, mathematics, geography, and history. On foundation-day he received a prize for distinction in Greek, the only prize he won for six years, although rewards of this sort were distributed pretty freely. In 1774, in his fifteenth year, he began the study of jurisprudence, but made no progress in it, partly because the subject did not interest him, partly

because of ill health,—for he was now growing fast, and
was frequently confined to bed, on one occasion for more
than a month. Some of the professors repeatedly complained to the Duke of his deficiencies, but in this
instance he was more keen-sighted than they. "Let
him alone," he said; "he is a youth who will come to
something." Although backward in his professional
studies, Schiller had already entered the path on which
he was afterwards to achieve fame. When he joined
the Academy, his powers were still dormant; he had not
been there many months before some of them were
awakened to tumultuous activity. The reading of contemporary literature was strictly forbidden, but that, of
course, only made it the more attractive; and by some
chance Schiller obtained a copy of Klopstock's "Messiah." Nobody can now read this once famous epic;
but its overstrained enthusiasm formed a striking contrast
to the dulness of the versifiers who represented German
poetry at the time when its first cantos were published.
To Schiller it revealed a new world of passion, aspiration,
and conflict; and he immediately began to devise an
epic, conceived in the same exalted spirit, on Moses.
He also wrote two tragedies, one entitled "Absalom,"
another "The Christians," the latter apparently setting
forth the sufferings and heroism of the early martyrs. In
such efforts he was encouraged by several friends, who,
along with himself, formed a little society for the study
of poetry. Among these friends was Schiller's Ludwigsburg companion, Von Hoven, who had gone to the Solitude some time before him, and who heartily welcomed
his old schoolfellow. Another of the band was Petersen,
full of fun and frolic, endowed with a lively wit which

sparkled none the less brightly because of the frowns of
severe inspectors. A third friend of Schiller, Scharffenstein, was for a time the most valued of all. He won
Schiller's esteem by boldly resisting a harsh official, an
act of heroism which the young poet forthwith celebrated in high-sounding verses. Scharffenstein was the
dandy of the Academy, in which respect he differed
widely from Schiller, who was continually being lectured
for his awkward gait and the untidiness of his uniform.
All these comrades were strongly attached to Schiller, and
they seem to have recognised in rough outlines most of
the qualities for which he was afterwards distinguished.
He was particularly remarkable for the ardour of his
affections : if he gave his heart, he gave it with passion ;
if, on the other hand, he was seriously offended, his
whole soul was thrown into a storm of excitement. In
1778, when they were approaching manhood, Scharffenstein wounded him by some thoughtless sarcasms.
Schiller at once renounced his friendship ; and when
Scharffenstein wrote to him, protesting that there must
be a misunderstanding, he received an answer full of
extravagant reproaches and of sentimental pathos. Notwithstanding the force of his passions, Schiller was
known even at this early period to possess a resolute
will. If he set up a goal for himself, external obstacles
never prevented him from reaching it, although they
might compel him to make for it by indirect ways.

When the Academy was about to be established in
Stuttgart, the Duke instituted a medical " faculty ; "
and the pupils of other departments were asked whether
any of them would prefer to adopt the new study.
Schiller, who disliked jurisprudence more and more,

gladly took advantage of this offer; and the decision
marked an epoch in his career. Among the teachers
whose lectures he now attended was Professor Abel, a
man of a noble temper, thoughtful and sympathetic.
His department included lectures on psychology, moral
philosophy, and æsthetics, on all of which he discoursed
with insight. Schiller listened to him eagerly, and
learned almost by heart some of the text-books, especially
Ferguson's 'Moral Philosophy,' with notes by Garve, a
clear and suggestive writer of that time. He did not,
however, abandon poetry. It was the custom of Professor Abel, in describing conflicts between the passions
and between passion and duty, to illustrate his doctrines
by quotations from dramatic writings; and on one occasion, in 1776—that is, when Schiller was in his seventeenth year—he read a passage from "Othello" in
Wieland's translation. "Schiller was all ears," wrote
Abel long afterwards; "every feature of his face expressed the feeling with which he was penetrated; he
raised himself up and listened as if entranced. Scarcely
was the lecture finished when he begged me to give him
the book, and from this time forward he studied it with
uninterrupted enthusiasm." When the first tumult had
subsided, he was rather repelled by the coldness displayed, as he thought, in Shakespeare's readiness to allow
comic incidents to break in upon heartrending scenes.
"I was not then capable," he himself said at a later
period, "of understanding nature at first hand." Nevertheless, Shakespeare filled his mind with new ideas, and
stimulated all his energies. At this time young Germany admired Ossian almost as much as Shakespeare;
and Schiller not only read "Fingal" and the other

Ossianic poems, but often enchanted his friends by declaiming his favourite passages. Goethe's "Goetz von Berlichingen," too, profoundly impressed the young enthusiasts; and, like most other Germans of "the reading world," they shed many sentimental tears over "The Sufferings of Young Werther." They were also moved by Lessing's "Emilia Galotti," and by the "Julius of Taranto" of Leisewitz, a drama which is now almost forgotten, but which had force and animation enough to secure Lessing's warm praise. The writer, however, who influenced Schiller most deeply was Rousseau. For a long time the only world which existed for him was that of the great misanthropical philanthropist. He was fascinated by Rousseau's glowing pictures of "nature," and shared all his burning scorn for despotism and conventionality. Why had man been endowed with powers if all of them were not to be freely exercised? What reason could there be in the nature of things for the advantages heaped on one class and denied to another? And was it not the clear duty of humanity to destroy institutions and customs that had been handed down from degenerate ancestors, and to return to primitive simplicity and happiness? As Schiller asked himself these questions, he strained passionately against the fetters by which he was bound, and yearned to take his part in the coming struggle for freedom. The Duke would have been considerably astonished if he could have guessed at the strange tempestuous life which was agitating the young pupil who seemed so quiet. Schiller had passed by a bound into a new world, and in this new world he was to achieve his first efforts in literature.

Stirred to ambition by the poets whom they adored,
their hearts all aglow with fiery passions, Schiller
and his comrades seized every opportunity for giving
expression to their struggling thoughts. Schiller far
surpassed the others in the height and range of his
activity. For some time he could not find a subject
offering full scope for imagination and feeling; but at
last the scheme of a tragedy, suggested by the suicide
of a student, suddenly flashed upon him. In furious
haste he dashed off scene after scene; but when completed it did not please him, and he threw it into the
fire. "The Student of Nassau," he had called it;
and in later years he regretted that it had been destroyed, as he felt sure that a drama written with so
much youthful ardour could not be without merit. He
also destroyed another tragedy, "Cosimo de' Medici,"
which, according to Petersen, closely resembled "Julius
of Taranto" in plan, and was not inferior to it in vigour
of conception. In addition to these dramatic efforts
Schiller wrote various lyrics, some of which were printed
in the 'Swabian Magazine,' with commendatory notices
by the editor, Herr Haug, a professor in the Academy,
and father of one of Schiller's fellow-students. One of
the lyrics thus published was "The Conqueror" ("Der
Eroberer"), a wild poem, in which he storms against the
wickedness of tyrants. His manner of composing these
early works cannot be cited in illustration of Words-
worth's doctrine that poetry is "emotion remembered in
tranquillity;" he wrote in a fever of excitement, breathing hard, and stamping his feet. Even in mature life
he could seldom sit quietly at his desk. He preferred
to stand, bending over the paper in an uneasy posture;

and when not writing he would restlessly walk about the room.

Early in 1778 Schiller saw that he must attend more seriously to his medical studies, and for about two years afterwards he wrote hardly any poetry. In science he now made rapid progress, being especially distinguished in the classes for anatomy and physiology. After the examination of 1778 he was classed in anatomy with the prizeman, to whom the prize fell by lot; and in 1779 he carried off three prizes. The day on which he obtained these small distinctions was made memorable to him by the presence of an illustrious visitor. The Duke of Weimar and Goethe happened to pass through Suttgart on their way back from Switzerland, and were cordially welcomed by Duke Karl Eugen, who was glad to exhibit to two such men an institution in which he took justifiable pride. On foundation-day they stood beside him as the prizes were distributed, the Duke of Weimar on the right hand, Goethe on the left. Goethe was then thirty years of age, in the flush of manly strength and beauty. He was naturally an object of profound interest to the better class of students; and we may suppose that Schiller (who was only ten years his junior) looked at him with more admiration than any one else, and perhaps with something of envy.

Schiller had hoped that 1779 would be his last year at the Academy. His wish, however, was not gratified. Before leaving the Academy he had to write a medical dissertation, and he had chosen as his theme "Philosophy and Physiology." Some of the examiners saw in this essay evidence of remarkable talent; others complained of an excess of rhetoric, and were scandalised by the boldness with which he attacked so high an authority as Haller. The Duke read the dissertation, and predicted (what he is not known to have done in any other instance) that the author would become "a very great subject;" but he announced at the same time that Schiller "must remain another year in the Academy, where his fire might be a little damped." With a heavy heart Schiller was obliged to submit to this decision.

His last year at the Academy—1780—was one of great unhappiness. Every restriction on his liberty irritated him; and his mind was charged with a tempest of titanic wrath against the wrongs of the world—those which he knew of, and still more, perhaps, those which he only imagined. Sometimes he was overcome by melancholy, and would gladly, or thought he would gladly, have shuffled off the mortal coil. "I am not yet twenty-one," he wrote to the father of one of his fellow-students who had recently died, a younger brother of Von Hoven; "but I may freely say that the world has no longer any charm for me : I take no pleasure in it; and the day of my departure from the Academy, which would have been a joyful day a few years ago, will not call forth from me a single cheerful smile. With every advance I make in years I become less and less happy ; the nearer I approach manhood the more I wish I had died in childhood. Were my life my own, I should be envious of the death of your dear son; but it belongs to my mother and to my three sisters, who without me would be helpless; for I am the only son, and my father begins to have grey hairs."

In this alternately sad and rebellious humour he had

to prepare for his final examinations. He wrote two
dissertations, one in Latin, the other in German. The
subject of the latter was "The Relation of the Animal
Nature of Man to his Spiritual Nature;" and it affords
ample proof that he had not only profited largely by the
instructions of his professors, but had made the relations
of mind and body a subject of much original study. It
might have been supposed that one whose tendencies
were of so ideal a character would try to assert the independence of mental operations; but what he does is
to indicate different ways in which they are awakened
and limited by physical causes. The essay was thought
to be worthy of publication, and was issued with a letter
expressing the author's gratitude to the Duke.

There are several illustrative quotations in this dissertation, and among them one from what professes to be an
English work, " Life of Moor, Tragedy by Krake." " Life
of Moor," as his friends knew, was " The Robbers."   In
writing this drama, which was soon to reveal to Germany
that a new force had arisen in her literature, he found
relief from the petty despotism against which he now so
vehemently rebelled.   The subject is said to have been
suggested by an incident recorded in the 'Swabian
Magazine' in 1775 ; and some parts of the tragedy
were probably written in 1777.   The work as a whole,
however, was produced in his last year at the Academy.
In order to obtain opportunities of writing, he sometimes remained all day in his room under pretence of
illness ; and occasionally he applied for admission to
the Academy hospital, where night-lights were burned.
If he heard any one approaching, he thrust his manuscript beneath a medical book, which he had always

conveniently at hand. The play was not completed in
the order in which it stands : he preferred to give form
to the conceptions by which his imagination happened
to be stirred at the moment of writing. Each scene,
when finished, was read to his friends, who stimulated
him by unstinted applause. On one occasion he was
loudly declaiming the appeal of Franz Moor to Moser at
the beginning of the fifth act—" Ha! what!—thou know-
est no worse crime than parricide ? Reflect ! on thy words
hang death, heaven, eternity, damnation ! "—when an
inspector, attracted by the noise, opened the door.
" Shame ! " cried this official, seeing Schiller storming
through the room,—" shame ! who would rage and curse
so ? " When he had gone, the listeners laughed, and
Schiller muttered, " A blockhead ! "

At last the day of deliverance came. On the 14th of
December 1780 the usual celebration took place, and
Schiller learned that he had received the appointment
of a regimental medical officer, with the comparatively
humble rank of " Feldscherer." This position did not
even entitle him to wear a sword as an officer, and he
left the Academy smarting under the consciousness of
ungenerous treatment.

Schiller had acquired at the Academy a rather formal,
military manner, which he retained throughout life. He
was very tall and slight, but with broad shoulders and
a full chest. While he remained in the army he wore
the usual pigtail, with stiff curls on either side of the
face ; but afterwards his long reddish hair fell freely
over his neck. His eyebrows were bushy, and the eyes,
which were of an uncertain colour—between light brown
and blue—had usually an expression of quiet thought-

fulness, but in conversation would sometimes glance brightly. Like his mother's eyes, they were delicate, and the eyelids were frequently inflamed. His forehead was broad and high, the chin prominent but well formed ; and the under lip, which was full and mobile, indicated every shade of passing feeling. A light blush easily passed over his features, which were pale, with a slight tinge of red on the cheeks. He laughed as heartily as a child, and everybody who met him remarked the kindness and gentleness of his smile.

CHAPTER III.

ABOUT two years after Schiller went to the Academy, his father was transferred to the Solitude as director of all the arrangements for the laying out of gardens and the planting of trees. He passed the remainder of his life happily in this position, and was ultimately raised, in recognition of his services, to the rank of major. The extent of his knowledge was manifested in a work which he published in 1795, and which went through two editions, on the art of the nursery gardener; but long before that time he was known as a master in his profession, and his methods were imitated not only in Würtemberg, but in many different parts of Germany. Every year he supplied large numbers of fruit-trees to foreign gardeners.

Before beginning his new duties, Schiller spent some pleasant days at the home of his parents. His sister, Christophine, was now a young woman of twenty-three, tall and handsome, and with some " accomplishments," of which the chief was a considerable aptitude for drawing. During this visit he had an opportunity for the first time of gaining the affections of his younger sisters,

Louise and Nanette—the latter a charming child of
three, her father's favourite.

Schiller was attached to the grenadier regiment of
General Augé in Stuttgart; and as most of the soldiers
were veterans, and rather sickly, plenty of work was
provided for him. From the outset he detested his
profession, and he does not seem to have been very
skilful, for he soon began to excite alarm by the extraordinary strength of the doses which he was in the habit
of administering. This peculiarity brought him into
frequent conflict with his superior, who was at last
obliged to issue orders that no prescription by the
young doctors under him should be attended to, unless
it had his signature. Notwithstanding his dislike of
his work, Schiller was for some time not unhappy : he
was now free, with all the world before him. Besides,
he had many friends—among them some of his old com-
panions at the Academy, who like himself were enjoying
the first delights of liberty. One of these, Scharffenstein, now a lieutenant, had written to Schiller and
"made up" their quarrel. Petersen was an assistant
librarian in Stuttgart, and of course placed at Schiller's
disposal the library with which he was connected. Von
Hoven had settled as a doctor at Ludwigsburg, but man-
aged to pay frequent visits to Stuttgart. These and
other friends often met in Schiller's room, where they
had much merry talk over exceedingly frugal suppers.
His room was sublet to him by a widow, Frau Vischer,
who was about thirty years of age, and, according to
most accounts, neither beautiful nor very intelligent.
Schiller, who was remarkably "susceptible," carried on
a Platonic flirtation with her, and she was the original

of the Laura whose virtues he celebrated in a series of famous odes.

For some time after Schiller settled in Stuttgart, he occupied most of his leisure in revising " The Robbers ; " and in April 1781 it was finished. Unfortunately no bookseller in Stuttgart would undertake to publish it. Petersen, who had occasion to go to Mannheim, took the manuscript with him, and Schiller wrote to him to spare no effort to find a publisher. Fifty gulden, he thought, he ought to be paid for it; anything beyond this would go to Petersen himself. " And hear," he continued,—" if you succeed, I will add a couple of bottles of Burgundy ! " Petersen, however, did not succeed, and in the end Schiller determined to have the play printed at his own expense. Some persons of his acquaintance being bold enough to become security for the necessary amount, the work was set about without delay ; and in July a little volume, remarkably well printed, appeared with this title-page—" Die Räuber. Ein Schauspiel. Frankfurt und Leipzig, 1781." This edition was published without the author's name.

Seldom has a work of genius made so profound an impression as was produced by " The Robbers." In a few weeks it was known far beyond the limits of Würtemberg ; and in Stuttgart Schiller became an object of universal curiosity and interest. Many respectable persons shook their heads at the dangerous tendencies of the young poet, but the youth of Germany enthusi-astically greeted him as the herald of a new and grander age. By-and-by travellers passing through Stuttgart would stop at his door, and beg to be allowed to talk with him ; and very much surprised some of them must

have been by the circumstances in which they found
him. The only furniture of his room was a table and
two benches. On the wall hung his clothes; and,
according to Scharffenstein, the visitors would see "in
one corner piles of 'The Robbers,' in another a quantity
of potatoes, with empty dishes, bottles, and such things."
"On every occasion," he adds, "a shy, silent review of
these objects would precede the conversation." He was
visited not only by lion-hunters, but by modest admirers
who sought his friendship; and one of these, Streicher, a
young musician, was soon to play a part that has gained
for him an honourable place in the record of Schiller's
life. During the public examinations at the Military
Academy in December 1780, Streicher had gone to
watch the proceedings,—mainly, perhaps, because the
day's work was often closed on these occasions by a
symphony conducted by the pupils. He was struck by
the vigour and animation with which a tall student with
reddish hair defended (in Latin) his dissertation against
a professor; and again, in the dining-hall, by the lively
and attractive manner of this same student as he con-
versed with the Duke, who leaned over his chair as if
he were a favourite. When "The Robbers" was being
everywhere talked about, Streicher strongly desired to
be introduced to the author. "His wish was fulfilled,"
he himself says, "and he was surprised to find in the
poet the youth whose first appearance had made so deep
an impression on him." To Streicher, Schiller's views
about everything, especially about music, seemed to be
"novel, convincing, and, at the same time, in the highest degree natural." His remarks on the works of other
writers were "striking, but charitable, and never ad-

vanced without evidence." "A personality so charming
and so amiable," he continues; "conversations which
raised the listener to his own level, ennobling every
feeling, adorning every thought; sentiments which manifested the purest goodness without weakness;—all this
could not but win the affection of a young artist of a
receptive temper, and add to the admiration with which
he had already regarded the poet the warmest attachment to the man."

To eke out his scanty pay, Schiller conducted for some
time a small weekly newspaper; and in association with
Petersen and his old friend and teacher, Professor Abel,
he started a quarterly periodical, 'The Würtemberg Re-
pertorium,' which was intended to be a complete review
of contemporary politics and literature.   Only three
numbers appeared; but one of these contained an admirable review, by Schiller himself, of "The Robbers,"
the defects as well as the merits of which he freely
discussed.   Another work reviewed by him in the 'Re-
pertorium' was 'The Anthology,' a collection of lyrical poetry which he himself had edited.   It originated
in Schiller's irritation at the manner in which he had
been treated by a Hérr Stäudlin, who had asked him to
contribute to a volume of verse.   Schiller had sent him
several poems, but he printed only one of them, and even
that was considerably mutilated.   Determined to punish
him for this impertinence, Schiller asked several of his
friends to help him in producing a volume which would
drive Stäudlin's book from the field.   As he advanced
in his undertaking he became interested in it for its own
sake, and contributed to it nearly all the best of his
early lyrics.   The volume (which he published at his

own expense) did not become widely known; but in
Würtemberg, and especially in Stuttgart, it added considerably to his fame as the most promising of the
younger poets of the time.

Meanwhile a great event in Schiller's life had occurred
—"The Robbers" had been produced on the stage. Soon
after it was published, he received a letter from Dalberg,
director of the Mannheim theatre, asking him to adapt
it for representation. Schiller was delighted by this
unexpected honour, and set to work immediately. On
Sunday, the 13th of January 1792, having started from
Stuttgart with the secret approval of his colonel, he
reached Mannheim in time for the first performance,
which was to begin at five o'clock. He found the theatre
crowded, for "The Robbers" was already so well known
that people had come from a great distance, some even
from Frankfort, to see it in its new form. The early
scenes hardly produced the effect which had been anticipated; but by-and-by the interest became intense, and it
expressed itself from time to time in bursts of vehement
applause. Never had a German play stirred such enthusiasm. The spectators dispersed with the conviction
that what they had seen was the appearance above the
horizon of a new star of the first magnitude.

After the play Schiller supped with the actors and
with Dalberg, all of whom congratulated him warmly
on his success. During the performance he had felt
strongly that the drama alone could open for him a
career adapted to his powers, and he expressed an ardent
wish that it might be possible for Dalberg to give him
permanent employment in connection with the Mannheim theatre. The prudent director, however, while

encouraging his aspirations, was careful not to commit himself by any definite promise. Next day Schiller started on his return journey, and, as he had given out that he was unwell, found on arriving at Stuttgart that his absence had not excited remark. He resumed his profession with a stronger dislike than ever of its dull routine, but he was made happy by the increasing fame of "The Robbers," which not only continued to be represented in Mannheim, but soon appeared in every important theatre in Germany.

Before the appearance of "The Robbers" on the stage, Schiller was already engaged on a new play, the subject of which was the conspiracy of Count Fiesco, a Genoese nobleman, against the Dorias. His attention had been drawn to this theme, while he was at the Academy, by a remark of Rousseau, to the effect that Fiesco was a character "worthy of the pencil of Plutarch." It is possible that the work may have been begun about the same time as "The Robbers," but the greater part of it was written in 1782. Schiller made a sincere attempt to master the characteristics of the age of the Dorias, consulting among other histories Robertson's 'Charles V.,' in which Fiesco's character is carefully sketched, and 'La Conjuration du Comte Jean-Louis de Fiesque,' by Cardinal Retz. For some time he made rapid progress, but his work was soon interrupted by formidable difficulties.

Among the friends who were attracted to him by "The Robbers" was Frau von Wolzogen, a lady of noble birth, whose son Wilhelm had been Schiller's fellow-student at the Academy. Both she and Frau Vischer often expressed a wish to see "The Robbers," and during the temporary absence of the Duke from Stuttgart, in May 1782, Schiller fancied that he might safely gratify their desire. All his longings for a life in accordance with his deepest sympathies were revived by this second visit to Mannheim, and he once more consulted Dalberg, who vaguely undertook to do "what was possible" on his behalf. After his return he was confined to bed by a severe attack of influenza, and during this period of solitude and reflection he seems to have finally decided to give up the medical profession, and to devote himself to literature. He wrote, therefore, to Dalberg, entreating him to use his influence with the Duke to secure his release—a request to which Dalberg considered it safest to make no answer.

By this time the two ladies had begun to whisper to their friends that they had visited Mannheim with Schiller, and the intelligence passed from one to another until it reached the ears of the Duke. He had read "The Robbers" with high displeasure, and now, summoning Schiller to his presence, sternly reprimanded him for writing a play at all, and especially such a play. As for his neglect of duty, that was an offence for which he would undergo fourteen days' arrest. Schiller bore his punishment meekly, but felt that he was rapidly approaching a crisis in which it would be necessary for him to act with vigour, or to consent to the destruction of his most cherished schemes. The crisis came sooner than he expected, for a controversy having arisen about a passage in "The Robbers" alluding to Grisons as "the Athens of modern swindlers," the matter was brought to the attention of the Duke, who immediately issued a peremptory order forbidding Schiller either to write books or to hold communication with foreigners. This order reached Schiller towards the end of August 1782, and a few days afterwards he addressed a respectful petition to the Duke, setting forth reasons why his liberty should not be so severely restricted. The petition was declined, and Schiller was commanded, on pain of arrest, to send no such documents in future to his sovereign.

If Schiller really intended to devote his energies to the drama, he had now no alternative but to fly from Stuttgart. There were some very powerful arguments in favour of submission; but his passion for the free play of his individual impulses was overmastering, and he was too sanguine not to hope that a bold stroke would be favoured by destiny. On the 17th of September a public welcome of unusual splendour was to be accorded to the Grand Duke Paul of Russia, and as it would be easy to slip out of Stuttgart unobserved on such an occasion, Schiller decided to depart on that day. The good Streicher, who had intended to go to Hamburg in the following spring to study under Bach, offered to accompany him, and the proposal was gladly accepted.

Schiller did not venture to tell his father of his plan, but his mother, his sister Christophine, and several of his most intimate friends, were let into the secret. On the day before his departure he walked to the Solitude, accompanied by Streicher and by Frau Meyer, the wife of the stage manager of the Mannheim theatre, who had treated him with much kindness. Captain Schiller could speak of nothing but the preparations for next day's ceremony—for the castle of the Solitude was to be brilliantly illuminated. While he was dilating on this subject Schiller quietly left the room with his mother, returning an hour afterwards with very inflamed eyes. On the morrow, at the appointed hour, Streicher called for Schiller's trunk, which was to have been packed and ready; but in arranging his books he had been attracted by an ode of Klopstock's, and for the moment the approaching journey was forgotten. Could he not write an ode at least as good? He would try; and, as Streicher entered, the last stanza was being finished. Streicher had to decide which was best,—Schiller's ode or Klopstock's; and he was, of course, too loyal not to give the verdict for his friend. At last the trunk was taken away; and at nine o'clock in the evening Schiller called for Streicher, to whom he solemnly displayed two rusty old pistols, which he carried under his cloak. Their carriage passed safely through the Esslinger Gate, where Scharffenstein was the officer on guard; and for an hour or two they drove on in silence. About midnight a turn in the road revealed the Solitude, splendidly lighted up. Schiller eagerly rose and pointed to the spot where his parents lived; but suddenly struck by a painful thought, he sank back in his seat, saying, with a sigh, "My mother!"

CHAPTER IV.

SCHILLER drove into Mannheim with a light heart, for
had he not the greater part of a new play in his pocket?
And if "The Robbers" had given him so wide a reputation, was it not certain that "Fiesco" would add lustre
to his name? Besides, was he not conscious of the
promptings of a lofty genius? and had the world ever
withheld its rewards from a bold and resolute spirit?
These anticipations were in the end fully justified, but
in the meantime he had entered upon an anxious and
troubled period, during which he was destined to sound
some of the profoundest depths of human misery.

As Dalberg had gone to Stuttgart to be present at the
ceremonies in honour of Grand Duke Paul, the two
friends called at once on the friendly manager, Meyer,
who, while much surprised to meet Schiller as a fugitive, gave him a hearty welcome, and found a suitable
lodging for him and his comrade. Schiller lost no time in
writing to the Duke, stating his reasons for what he had
done, and offering to return on condition that permission
were granted to him to continue his literary pursuits.
The letter was enclosed to an officer of high position,

his father's friend, who had influence at Court; but it was probably written rather for the purpose of softening his father's anger, than because he had the faintest hope of inducing the Duke to come to terms. The only answer he received was an intimation that he might safely return, as the Duke was in a particularly good humour.

Meanwhile "Fiesco" had been the subject of a good deal of conversation among the actors; and to give them an opportunity of estimating it, Meyer arranged that it should be read to them in his house. Schiller's experience on this occasion was much the same as that of Congreve, who read "The Old Bachelor" to the players so badly that they almost decided to reject it. The first act of "Fiesco" was listened to in silence, and after the second act most of the actors went away without expressing either praise or blame, but manifestly dissatisfied. Meyer took Streicher into another room, and anxiously asked whether he was certain that Schiller had written "The Robbers," for he had never heard a more wretched play than "Fiesco." Poor Schiller returned in a melancholy mood to his lodging, complaining that he was the victim of envy and malice; but fortunately Meyer had requested that the manuscript should be left with him, and next morning he received Streicher with a cry of joy. "Fiesco," he declared, was a masterpiece, even better than "The Robbers," and only Schiller's broad Swabian dialect and pompous declamation had prevented the players from recognising its worth. Streicher ran back with these glad tidings to his friend, whose sad broodings had kept him awake until far on in the morning.

It soon began to be reported in Mannheim that a demand would be addressed to the Elector of the Palatinate for the extradition of Schiller. He was therefore counselled to seek refuge elsewhere; and he and Streicher decided in the first instance to make for Frankfort. When they left Stuttgart their united wealth was fifty-one gulden; and as a considerable part of this small sum had already vanished, they were obliged to undertake the journey on foot. On a bright October afternoon they started, spending the first night at a village called Sandtorf. Next evening, after a walk of twelve hours, they reached Darmstadt very tired, and with but faint hopes to sustain their courage. All day Schiller had trudged along, speaking seldom, and hardly even stopping to admire the beautiful scenery unless his attention were called to it by his companion. On the third day Schiller was so exhausted that he had to lie down in a wood, where happily he fell fast asleep, faithful Streicher keeping watch by his side. When he had slept two hours, some one whom Streicher took for a recruiting officer came along and stopped to look at them. "Who are you?" he asked. "Travellers," loudly answered Streicher, who did not like the man's appearance, and was anxious that they should resume their journey. Schiller awoke refreshed; and in a short time they found themselves in Frankfort, where they hired a room in an inn opposite the Maine bridge, coming to precise terms with the landlord as to the cost of their poor lodging and meagre fare.

In the morning Schiller wrote to Dalberg, fully explaining his circumstances, and asking him to advance 100 gulden. He had incurred heavy debts in Stuttgart, and this sum would at least enable him to give his creditors some evidence of honest intentions. The request was not extravagant, for he had received nothing for "The Robbers" except his travelling expenses when he went to see it; and he had every reason to expect that the theatre would profit largely by "Fiesco." By-and-by a letter came from Meyer, containing Dalberg's answer. "Fiesco" in its existing form was pronounced to be unsuited for the stage, and the director added that he could not advance money. Schiller uttered not a word when he read this crushing decision; but Streicher understood his agitation by his pale face and quivering lip. The whole basis of his expectations had been swept away, and he seemed to have nothing before him but ruin.

He had in his possession a poem on which he set high value, and, driven by necessity, he took it to a bookseller, to whom he offered it for twenty-five gulden. The bookseller was willing to give eighteen gulden; but even in his poverty the proud poet would not part with his work on terms which he considered inadequate. Fortunately Streicher received from his mother an instalment of the money which had been set apart for his journey to Hamburg; and with this they started for Worms, where they found another letter from Meyer, making an appointment to meet them at an inn in Oggersheim, a village near Mannheim. Here they were cordially received by the kind manager, his wife, and two friends; and a long consultation followed as to Schiller's plans. Meyer had no doubt that if certain alterations were made in "Fiesco," it would be accepted; and it was finally arranged that Schiller should remain with Streicher in Oggersheim (the one as Dr Schmidt, the other as Dr Wolf) until the work was done,—which it would be, he thought, in about three weeks.

At this period, however, Schiller found it hard to work according to a strictly defined plan; he could not force his thoughts into one channel if they persistently sought to flow in another. Now his imagination had been for some time kindled by a conception which, he hoped, would far surpass his previous efforts. This was the scheme of the play which ultimately received the title of "Intrigue and Love" ("Kabale und Liebe"), but which at first he called "Luise Miller." It was to be a tragedy of middle-class life, and seemed to provide many opportunities for outbursts of stormy passion and for scenes of tender pathos. Two of the three weeks which were to be given to "Fiesco" he devoted to the new play; and so completely did it absorb his energies, that for days he would not go out even for a short walk. His imagination was especially alert in the evening, when he would pace his room by twilight or by moonlight — Streicher both stimulating and soothing him with music. To these peaceful hours he looked forward every day with pleasure, and at their mid-day meal he would say to Streicher, "You will play to me this evening?"

At last Schiller forced himself to return to "Fiesco," and it was soon despatched to Dalberg. But he was again doomed to disappointment : after considerable delay, Dalberg decided that the play was still likely to be ineffective. Schiller had been writing of his prospects in sanguine terms to his parents and his sister; and he had tried to persuade himself that success was within easy reach. Now he was driven almost to despair. His creditors had become clamorous, and his father was too poor to undertake fresh burdens; while Streicher had so completely exhausted his resources, that he was compelled to accept employment as a musician in Mannheim. In addition to these troubles, Schiller was in some alarm for his safety; for the Duke of Würtemberg had ordered him to return, and it was by no means improbable that he would become the subject of negotiations between the Würtemberg and the Palatinate Governments. He wrote, therefore, to his friend, Frau von Wolzogen, reminding her that she had once offered him an asylum in her house in Bauerbach, and asking her if he might now take advantage of her kindness. Frau von Wolzogen had three sons, whose prospects partly depended on the favour of the Duke; nevertheless, she at once assented to Schiller's request. Part of his reckoning at Oggersheim he had been able to discharge by selling his watch; he now paid the rest of it, and made some provision for his journey to Bauerbach, by disposing of " Fiesco " for ten louis-d'or. These arrangements made, Streicher, Meyer, and other friends agreed to meet him at Oggersheim, and to accompany him to Worms. On a clear, frosty night, under bright stars, they saw him mount the mail-coach, which, after two days' journey, was to take him to his remote place of refuge. To all of them he said a kindly adieu; but his feelings for Streicher were revealed by a firm hand-

grip, which was intended to say, and did say, infinitely
more than could have been expressed by the most elo-
quent of spoken farewells.[1]

Bauerbach is a village which consisted at that time of
about thirty houses, in the Thuringian Forest, within two
hours' walk of Meiningen. When Schiller arrived there
late in the evening of the 7th December 1782, snow
lay deep on the ground; and heartily glad he was to
find himself in a well-warmed room, for (as his friends
remembered with remorse after parting from him) he
had been very insufficiently clad for a long, cold journey.
For about eight months he resided (as Dr Ritter) in
Bauerbach; and visitors may still see his low-roofed
room, with his arm-chair, his table, and two old portraits of German princes on the walls. He often consoled himself in his loneliness by taking long walks
among the neighbouring hills, and sometimes he carried
a gun, although he was probably but a sorry sportsman.
Occasionally, too, he visited Meiningen, where he had at
least one friend, Reinwald, the keeper of the Ducal library,
to whom Frau von Wolzogen had given him a letter of
introduction. Reinwald was about forty-six years of age,
a man of profound learning, who, although of a naturally
kind disposition, had been made bitter and moody by
disappointment and ill health. He is a figure of some
importance in Schiller's biography, for they were destined to become near relatives. A letter of Schiller's

---

[1] Streicher lived afterwards in Vienna as a pianoforte-maker. The
romance of his life was the recollection of his relation to Schiller, after
whose death he published a bright little book—'Schiller's Flight
from Stuttgart' ('Schillers Flucht aus Stuttgart')—giving a full
account of their adventures.

sister, Christophine, falling accidentally into Reinwald's hands, he read it; and being much pleased by her good sense, and by the warmth of her affection for her brother, he wrote to her and ultimately asked her to marry him. Schiller was sincerely attached to Reinwald, but thought that his age and the peculiarities of his temper would make him an unsuitable husband for his sister. She, however, thought differently; and in 1786 she was united to her elderly lover, who, until his death thirty years afterwards, found her a patient, considerate, and affectionate wife.

Work was always difficult for Schiller unless he had frequent intercourse with congenial minds; but he forced himself to go on with "Luise Miller," and he also began "Don Carlos." Towards the end of 1782 his solitude was interrupted by a visit from Frau von Wolzogen and her daughter Charlotte, who remained for nearly a month. Charlotte, who was about sixteen, fascinated Schiller by her brightness, grace, and amiability, and he soon began to form glorious visions in which she played the leading part as the bride of a happy and famous poet. He did not conceal his hopes from Frau von Wolzogen; but she discouraged them, for she saw that he could not for a long time be in circumstances which would justify him in marrying. Charlotte does not seem to have known how ardently he loved her, and in a few months she put an end for ever to his dream by giving her affections to some one else. In Frau von Wolzogen herself, who was still comparatively young, and remarkable for her quick intelligence and generous impulses, Schiller found one of the most sympathetic of friends; and his letters to her after her departure were full of almost passionate expressions of attachment and admiration.

In May 1783 his friends were once more at home, and Schiller was so happy in their society that he often proclaimed his intention of spending his life in Bauerbach. Frau von Wolzogen was too much his friend to approve of so wild a scheme; and one summer afternoon, while they were walking in a wood, she ventured to suggest to him that it might be worth while to visit Mannheim to find out what were likely to be the chances of "Luise Miller." Some months before, Dalberg had written to him, indicating a wish to renew their friendly relations. Schiller replied rather coldly, as if the Mannheim theatre were indifferent to him; but Dalberg, who knew the value of the author of "The Robbers," wrote again, saying that Schiller's new play could not be in his hands too soon. To Frau von Wolzogen it seemed that this opportunity should not be neglected; and Schiller was obliged to confess that he would probably benefit by coming into contact with "the world." The result of their conversation was, that in the last days of July 1783, Schiller was again in Mannheim, having gone with the full intention of speedily returning to Bauerbach. His friend supplied him with money for the journey, and unfortunately he had already increased his debts by borrowing considerable sums either directly from her or from others in her name.

Dalberg happened to be in the country; but after his return, in about a fortnight, he received Schiller courteously, and expressed his conviction not only that "Luise Miller" would succeed, but that "Fiesco" might be made a good acting play. In a short time he asked Schiller to accept a formal engagement as the dramatist of the Mannheim theatre. Schiller would still have preferred to live at Bauerbach; but feeling that it was his imperative duty to take any honourable position in which he might hope to escape from his difficulties, he accepted Dalberg's offer. The terms were that, besides giving an opinion on any works that might be submitted to him, he should, within a year, prepare " Fiesco " and " Luise Miller " for the stage, and supply another play. In return for these services he was to receive 300 gulden, of which 200 gulden were to be advanced immediately; he was also to have the right of printing his dramatic works, and each play was to be represented once for his benefit. Schiller's tendency was always to overrate the advantages of a new arrangement, and he now persuaded himself that he was about to enter upon a career of uninterrupted prosperity. His parents were informed of his altered prospects, and he was much pleased to receive the warm congratulations of his mother and sister.

When he signed the contract with Dalberg, he was suffering from a severe attack of ague, which prevailed at that time in Mannheim, and of which, to Schiller's deep regret, his old friend Meyer died. For many months he was unable to get rid of this disorder, but he continued to work at " Fiesco," which was ready before the end of 1783. The changes on which Dalberg insisted did not commend themselves to Schiller's judgment; they not only involved a wide departure from the facts of history, but made the conclusion of the play tame and cold. The first representation took place in January 1784, and although several scenes were not without

effect, the work as a whole excited little interest. About
three months later, " Luise Miller," which had received
the title of " Kabale und Liebe," was produced ; and
the enthusiasm with which it was applauded amply com-
pensated Schiller for the comparative failure of " Fiesco."

Before the close of 1783 he had received a token of
his growing fame by being made a member of the German Society, a well-known literary body in Mannheim,
under the protection of the Elector Palatine. After admission each member had to read a dissertation, and
Schiller chose as his subject, " The Theatre as a moral
institution." This paper he soon afterwards considered
very inadequate, but it contains the germs of some of
the principles which he ultimately set forth in his philosophical writings. It was not read until June 1784,
and by that time all the glowing hopes with which he
had undertaken his new duties had vanished. His
health was still bad, and he had permanently injured it
by taking excessive quantities of cinchona-bark. Even
more distressing than his prolonged illness were the
anxieties caused by his poverty. The lives of many
German men of letters have been embittered by sordid
care, but few have been in such constant straits as
Schiller during these early years. After receiving two-
thirds of his salary he soon drew the remaining third ;
and in lieu of " benefits " Dalberg gave him 200 gulden.
These sums might perhaps have sufficed for ordinary
expenses, but his debts he had no means of discharging.
Driven to bay, he appealed to his father, who was now
becoming old, and felt that his first duty was to his wife
and daughters. It is painful to read the correspondence
of father and son, neither of whom was perfectly just to

the other—the son making demands which could not be complied with, the father responding with reproaches which were certainly not altogether deserved.

In August 1784 Schiller's connection with the Mannheim theatre came to an end, Dalberg having apparently thought that his genius was exhausted. It had often occurred to Schiller that perhaps he ought to resume his old profession; but happily he hit upon a device which was more in accordance with his inclinations. This was the plan of issuing a periodical, to be published once in two months. The scheme was taken up with his usual eagerness, and on the 11th of November 1784 he printed an advertisement setting forth in a lofty and self-confident tone the great results which he hoped to achieve. The name he selected for the new miscellany was 'The Rhenish Thalia.' " The public," he wrote, " is now everything to me,—my study, my sovereign, my confidant. To it alone I wholly belong. Before this tribunal, and before no other, I will place myself. This only I fear and reverence. I am conscious of something great in the idea of wearing no fetters except the judgment of the world, of appealing to no throne except the human mind." During the winter of 1784-85 he worked hard at 'Thalia,' but with all his efforts he could not produce the first number before March 1785.

Schiller had many friends in Mannheim, and one of the chief of these was Schwan the bookseller, to whom he had sold " Fiesco." Schwan had a daughter of about nineteen years of age, Margareta, a clever, genial, and attractive girl, on whom had devolved after her mother's death all the responsibilities of housekeeping. Charlotte von Wolzogen being unattainable,

Schiller cultivated Margareta's friendship; and although
she was of a coquettish temper and often provoked him,
he soon passed from friendship to love, and hoped that
she might become his wife. At this period, however,
he was not a very trustworthy lover; and it happened that, while he was undecided whether or not to
ask Schwan's permission to woo his daughter, he met a
lady who acquired an extraordinary ascendancy over
him. This was Charlotte von Kalb, a woman of position and fortune, the wife of a major in the French
army for whom she had not much affection. She was
about two years younger than Schiller, slightly built,
very beautiful, with dark hair, and eyes of a deep brown
that lighted up as she spoke. Her gestures were animated, and she delighted in expressing bold and para-
doxical opinions. Her imagination was so active and
so wayward, that, according to Herder, it prevented her
from ever "seeing reality;" and a passing whim would
plunge her from a mood of rapturous happiness into
profound gloom, or exalt her with equal suddenness
from gloom to happiness again. This strange creature,
changeful as the aspects of an April sky, visited Mannheim in the spring of 1784, bringing with her a letter
of introduction from Reinwald to Schiller, of whose
writings she was a warm admirer. In autumn she returned with the intention of remaining for some time,
her husband being stationed with his regiment in
Landau, and going to see her several times a-week.
By-and-by Schiller came completely under her spell,
and she loved him with all the vehemence of her passionate nature. To Frau von Kalb life appeared for the
first time to be thoroughly worth living; but to Schiller

their relation was a source of constant disquietude and vexation. He was drawn towards her by an irresistible charm, yet he was never at rest in her presence; and when he again became master of himself he confessed that "her influence over him had not been salutary." That she exerted influence over him, however, is not surprising; for, long afterwards, Jean Paul Richter was almost as enthusiastic as Schiller had been about her "great eyes" and "great soul," and her society was sought by Goethe, Herder, and Fichte.

Through Frau von Kalb's influence Schiller was invited, towards the end of 1784, to read some passages from his writings at the Court of Hesse-Darmstadt. He chose the first act of "Don Carlos," which was received with the highest favour. Among the company was Duke Karl August of Weimar, Goethe's friend; and he was so pleased with what he heard that he entered into conversation with Schiller, asking him minutely about his circumstances and prospects. Next day Schiller received from the Duke of Weimar a brief note conferring on him the title of Rath (Councillor). This was but a small honour; but it made Schiller very happy, for he took it as an indication that he might look for more substantial benefits from one to whom German literature was already deeply indebted. In the meantime, however, these benefits did not come; and as winter advanced he almost lost hope, not knowing in what direction to turn for aid.

In June 1784, Schiller received a packet which he opened with considerable curiosity. It came from Leipsic, and contained a letter expressing the warmest admiration for his writings, and thanking him for their high ideal tone. The letter was signed by C. G. Körner, Minna and Dora Stock, the daughters of a well-known engraver (the former betrothed to Körner), and L. F. Huber. Along with the letter were portraits of the four friends, drawn with silver point on parchment by Dora, a silk letter-case, beautifully embroidered by Minna, and one of Schiller's poems set to music by Körner. Schiller had never been more touched than by this spontaneous manifestation of goodwill; yet he made no answer for six months, probably because he was too depressed to respond in a perfectly genial spirit. When at last he wrote, he received a prompt reply; and in his misery it flashed upon him soon afterwards, Why not go to Leipsic and be near these sincere and sympathetic friends? "Oh," he wrote, "my soul pants after new nourishment, after better men—after friendship, attachment, love. I must go to you; I must learn to have joy in my own heart again, and give a lively impulse to my whole being by the most intimate intercourse with you. My poetic vein stagnates; you must give it warmth again. Near you I shall be twice, thrice what I once was—and more than that, my best friends, I shall be happy."

Of the correspondents thus addressed, Körner was the leading spirit, and fortune was indeed gracious to Schiller in providing him at such a time with such a friend. Körner is now, perhaps, most widely known as the father of the young poet who in the war of liberation kindled the enthusiasm of the German armies by his patriotic songs; but his relation to Schiller gives him a solid title for his own sake to affection and respect. He was Schiller's senior by about three years, and had already made his mark as a lawyer. To literature and philosophy he had devoted much attention; he was also an accomplished musician; and his good sense, kindness, and vivacity caused him to be a universal favourite in the society in which he moved. It gave him deep pleasure to find that a poet whom he admired was likely to value his friendship, and he accordingly encouraged Schiller to carry out his design of visiting Leipsic. But he did much more. Having about this time invested a considerable sum in the business of a well-known Leipsic bookseller, Göschen, he was able to induce the latter to offer to undertake the publication of 'Thalia' on terms advantageous to Schiller, and he willingly advanced a loan of 300 thalers. There was, therefore, a sudden break in the clouds which had so long been gathering; and after the issue of the first number of 'Thalia,' Schiller took advantage of the gleam of unexpected sunshine, and stepped cheerfully forward to new destinies. By his departure from Mannheim, early in April 1785, he closed, without being aware of it, a distinct period of his career. During this period he had passed through many struggles and endured much pain, but he had also done work of sustained excellence, and his genius had been disciplined and strengthened for still loftier flights.

CHAPTER V.

SCHILLER'S EARLY WRITINGS.

At the time when Schiller entered upon his career as a man of letters, German literature had already begun to manifest those new energies and impulses which were to make it for a period the most important literature in Europe. For more than a century the mind of the nation had slumbered, producing in philosophy alone, thanks to the penetrating genius of Leibnitz, any worthy contribution to the intellectual life of the world. In literature it had been content with feeble imitations of foreign models, chiefly French; the drama being, perhaps, more than any other species of imaginative effort, subject to French influence. The appearance of the opening cantos of Klopstock's "Messiah" was the first decisive indication that the German genius was about to contend on equal terms with its rivals; for, with all his faults, Klopstock had imagination, force, and courage. Wieland struck out in an opposite direction, and by his light epicureanism, his quiet irony, and his mastery of a graceful style, he did quite as much as Klopstock to foster an independent spirit among the writers of the new generation. Important as was the influence of

Wieland and Klopstock, however, it pales before that of
Lessing, who, while preparing the way for those who
were to come after him, did work which is as valuable
to-day as it was in the eighteenth century. By his
dramas, his controversies, and his original and powerful
criticism, he evoked higher ideals than had ever before
been presented to his countrymen, and encouraged his
successors to have confidence in the free exercise of their
own powers. The current of thought and aspiration,
of which Lessing was the leading representative, was
deepened by a growing acquaintance with Greek and
English poetry, and by that mighty agitation in France,
which in politics was making for the Revolution, in literature for the Romantic school. German literature was
not, of course, directly affected by Frederick the Great;
but indirectly it received a strong impetus from the
revival of patriotic ardour, which was due to his heroic
conflict with more than half of the civilised world.

Had the literary movement advanced on the lines
traced by Lessing, it would have combined freedom with
a frank recognition of the eternal laws of art. In the
first flush of youthful activity, however, it seemed to
those who inherited his task that liberty was incompatible with law in any form. They were deeply dissatisfied
with the world and with themselves; society as it existed, with its countless anomalies in the distribution of
happiness, in religion, in thought, had become hateful to
them; and they panted for a life which, being without
restraint, should be one prolonged rapture. The expression of their glowing passions could not, they supposed,
be adequate, if it were not vehement and stormy; and so
Germany was startled by the wild cries of the " Sturm

und Drang" poets. Lessing turned in disgust from a
ferment of contending elements which were so opposed
to his chastened vigour; and he was not altogether without excuse for the melancholy conviction that all his
labour had been in vain. His failure, however, was
only in appearance, for among the "Sturm und Drang"
poets was Goethe; and as the movement was splendidly
opened by "Goetz von Berlichingen" and "Werther,"
so it was destined to be splendidly closed by "The Robbers" and "Intrigue and Love."

In his Essay on Sir Walter Scott, Keble contends that
"poetry is the indirect expression in words, most appropriately in metrical words, of some overpowering emotion, or ruling taste, or feeling, the direct indulgence
whereof is somehow repressed." Whatever may be said
of this as an exhaustive definition of poetry, it exactly
applies to Schiller's early dramas. When they were
written, his "overpowering emotion" was one of fierce
resistance to the order of the world, as he knew it. An
ideal of the world as it ought to be, he had not; but
that the dignity of human nature was obscured by unjust laws, and by still more unjust conventions, of this
he was sure; and the belief filled him, not only with
pity for those whom unjust laws and conventions oppressed, but with rage against the system that oppressed
them. For these feelings, intensified, in the first instance, by his own sufferings as the victim of crushing rules at the Academy, and afterwards by his hardships as a fugitive from a threatening despot, there could
be no sufficient outlet except in literature; and in his first
plays he poured them forth with an energy which is un-
surpassed, perhaps unmatched, in any of his later works.

Of these three plays, all of which are in prose, "The Robbers" is the most remarkable. Almost every scene, it is true, contains extravagant passages, and some of the figures are rather guesses at character than living forms. The hero, Karl Moor, is, however, a creation of true genius. When he is first introduced, we find him uttering the sort of thoughts and sentiments that might be expected from an ardent disciple of Rousseau. "Laws," he declares, "have never formed a great man," but freedom produces "men of colossal type." "Oh," he cries, "that the spirit of Arminius still glowed in the ashes! Give me an army of lads such as I am, and Germany would become a republic, compared with which it would be said that Rome and Sparta were convents." While he is in this violent humour, longing for heroic action, he receives a letter from his brother, Franz Moor, telling him that he is disowned by his father, and that, if he returns to his home, he will be thrown into the deepest dungeon of the castle. He is stung almost to madness by this injustice. Now, more than ever, he is persuaded of the hatefulness of society. Civilisation seems to him a vast structure based on wrong, and he will assault it with furious energy. He forms his comrades into a robber band, and with them wars against every institution which men hold in respect, determined that outraged nature shall at last have her due. No other German drama presents so striking a picture of desolating force. By the might of his resistless will, Moor asserts absolute supremacy over his followers, and he passes from violence to violence, each more terrible than the last, shrinking from no scene of horror to which his destiny appears to call him. Yet he never altogether loses our sympathy, for his passions are those of a mind radically generous, and in his most monstrous actions he is thinking not of his own welfare but of what he supposes to be the welfare of the miserable and the enslaved. Still more powerful, however, and touching deeper facts of human nature, are the scenes in which he at last begins to doubt whether the end he has in view justifies the means, and whether in any case he has a sure title to the character he has assumed. Ultimately his doubts are changed into certainty, and he closes his career by rendering himself to justice, feeling, when it is too late, that his methods of destroying the elements of life which he loathes are infinitely worse than these elements themselves. The interest of the play culminates in the famous second scene of the third act, where, for the first time, he sees the struggle in which he is engaged in its true light. The robbers have defeated, after a desperate fight, an apparently overwhelming force, and they are now encamped on a height, among trees, in the neighbourhood of the Danube. The sun is setting, and Karl Moor is gazing at it intently.

"*Schwarz.* How splendidly the sun sets!

Moor (fascinated by the scene). So dies a hero—adorable!

Grimm. You appear to be deeply moved.

Moor. When I was still a child, it was my favourite thought to live like the sun, to die like it (*with suppressed pain*). It was a boyish thought!

Grimm. I will hope so.

Moor (pressing his hat over his face). There was a time—leave me alone, comrades.

Schwarz. Moor! Moor!—the deuce! How his colour changes!

Grimm. The devil! What is wrong? Is he ill?

Moor. There was a time when I could not sleep if I had forgotten my prayers——

Grimm. Are you mad? Will you let yourself be tutored by the years of your boyhood?

Moor (leaning his head on Grimm). Brother! brother!

Grimm. How? Be not a child, I pray you——

Moor. Were I but a child! Were I but a child again!

Grimm. Pooh, pooh!

Schwarz. Cheer up! See what a picturesque landscape—what a lovely evening!

Moor. Yes, friends; this world is so beautiful!

Schwarz. Come, that was well said.

Moor. The earth is so splendid!

Grimm. Right, right! that is what I like to hear.

Moor (self-absorbed). And I so hideous in this beautiful world—and I a monster on this splendid earth!

Grimm. Oh! oh!

Moor. My innocence! my innocence! See! everything goes out to sun itself in the peaceful ray of spring—why do I alone draw hell from the joys of heaven? Everything is so happy, all things are so united by the spirit of peace! The whole world one family, and a Father above—but not *my* Father; I alone the rejected—I alone driven from the ranks of the pure; not for me the sweet name of child; never for me the yearning glance of the beloved one; never, never the embrace of the bosom friend. *(Turning wildly round.)* Encircled by murderers; vipers hissing around me; bound to crime by iron fetters; on the bending reed of crime hanging dizzily over the pit of perdition; amid the flowers of the happy world a howling Abbadona![1]

Schwarz (to the others). Extraordinary! I have never seen him thus.

Moor (sadly). Oh that I might return to my mother's womb! that I might be born a beggar! I would ask no more, oh

---

[1] Abbadona is one of the fallen angels in Klopstock's "Messiah." He alone of the rebels repents.

heaven !—that I might become like one of these day-labourers ! Oh, I would work until blood rolled from my temples to purchase the rapture of one hour of mid-day slumber, the blessedness of a single tear !

Grimm (to the others). Patience ! The paroxysm is passing.

Moor. There was a time when tears so readily flowed ! Oh, ye days of peace ! Oh, castle of my father, ye green, enchanting valleys ! Oh, all ye elysian scenes of my childhood ! will ye never more return ? never, with gentle breezes, cool my burning breast ? Mourn with me, nature ! They will never more return, never with gentle breezes cool my burning breast. Gone ! gone ! Irrecoverable ! "

While Karl Moor supposes that he is bitterly wronged by his father, the old man continues to love him, and longs for his return. The agent of his ruin is his gloomy, selfish, and unscrupulous brother. Having despatched the letter which drives Karl to despair, Franz Moor tries to force the affections of Amalia, his brother's betrothed, and ultimately seizes the estates, throwing the elder Moor into a dungeon, where he is supposed to die. Secretly, however, the father is saved by the fidelity of an old servant ; and Amalia remains true to her absent lover. Reminded of the past by the adventures of a youth who falls into his hands, Karl visits his home without immediately revealing himself ; and the visit results in the discovery of his brother's villany. His father dies when Karl confesses himself to be a brigand, and Franz, who is about to be seized, takes his own life amid the flames of the burning castle. In despair Amalia appeals to the robbers to end her misery by death, and Karl himself slays her, exclaiming, " Moor's beloved shall die only by Moor's hand ! "

In developing this wild plot, Schiller indulges in a vast amount of boyish rant, and many of the speeches could not now be listened to seriously. A strong impression is produced by one scene, in which Franz Moor, in conversation with Pastor Moser, to still the rising fears of conscience, sets forth a base materialistic philosophy. Here Schiller was expressing thoughts with which he had come into contact in his studies, and he penetrates deeply into the recesses of a spirit striving to evade its responsibilities by sophistry, by which it is only half convinced. In almost every other scene Franz Moor is a mere monster, put together, apparently, in imitation of Richard III., and Edmund in "King Lear," but without any trace of their vitality. Hardly any attempt is made to give a definite character to the elder Moor, and there is little truth to nature in the presentation of Amalia, who, instead of acting for her lover, as the scheme of the play would easily have permitted her to do, wastes her force in vague sentimental declamation. She does not even recognise him when he visits the castle, although others soon penetrate through his disguise. None of these defects, however, obscure the high imaginative energy displayed in Karl Moor and his followers. The robbers subject to Moor are cast in a rougher mould than their chief, and have not his wide, revolutionary aims; but they share his love of freedom, and each bears the stamp of a strong and clearly marked individuality.

In creative force Schiller's next play, " The Conspiracy of Fiesco " ("Die Verschwörung des Fiesco "), is far below the level of "The Robbers." After making himself, by a brilliant stroke, master of the Genoese Republic, the Fiesco of history met with a sudden death. He was going on board a vessel when the plank on which he was crossing gave way; and being heavily armed, he sank and was drowned. An accident of this kind, however impressive in real life, is not a fit basis for tragedy; and Schiller, being well aware of the fact, was compelled to deprive Fiesco's death of its accidental character. The means which he devised was to represent his hero as influenced in part by motives of personal ambition. One of Fiesco's confederates, Verrina, is represented as a man of pure republican sympathies; and when the conspiracy has been conducted to a triumphant issue, Verrina entreats his chief to crown the work by establishing perfectly free government. Fiesco refuses to give the pledge demanded of him; whereupon Verrina avenges the cause of liberty by overturning the plank and plunging him into the sea. A genuinely tragic motive is thus, no doubt, provided; but it is at the expense of the character of Fiesco, who has no longer a claim to be regarded as a champion of republicanism. Even with such mingled impulses his character might perhaps have been made coherent; but, unfortunately, the greater part of the play was written before Schiller decided as to the manner in which he would end it. Thus he hesitates, all through, between two conceptions; they are not welded together in a figure of sure and distinct outlines. Verrina is consistent from first to last; but his position is subordinate, and he has no qualities by which we are either strongly attracted or repelled. It would have been difficult for Schiller to make the conspiracy seem natural by giving prominence to the grand character of Andrea Doria; he was therefore justified in laying stress mainly on the tyranny of Andrea's nephew, Gianettino. His effects are, however, too easily attained, since he attributes to Gianettino no acts or tendencies which mark him off from the most commonplace of brutal ruffians. Fiesco has a very beautiful wife, Leonore; and he masks his ultimate designs by pretending to neglect her and to pay court to Julia, Gianettino's sister. The character of Julia is made unnecessarily coarse; and we are perplexed by sudden and unexplained transitions in Leonore, who begins as a shy and retiring young wife and ends as a passionate enthusiast.

It was not surprising that Dalberg hesitated for some time to accept a play in which there are so many radical flaws; yet he could scarcely help seeing the excellence of its purely technical qualities. The action is more condensed than in "The Robbers;" there is less extravagance in the dialogue; the language, if not always so forcible, is keener and finer; and the defects of the scheme are often concealed by outbursts of impressive rhetoric. And one character, Muley Hassan, a Moor, whom Fiesco wins for his service by contemptuous generosity, has at least the merit of exuberant life. In the hands of a good actor, he seldom fails to strike a powerful note by his thoroughgoing rascality and rough humour.

In "Intrigue and Love" ("Kabale und Liebe"), Schiller again trusted solely to the imagination for his plot; and he was able once more, as in "The Robbers," to make the drama the reflection of his own stormy passions. The scene is laid in one of the petty German courts of the eighteenth century; and we almost wonder that there was not a German as well as a French Revolu-

tion, when we see the hatred and scorn with which
Schiller presents the heartlessness of the higher classes,
and their cynical contempt for every one beneath their
own rank. The heroine, Luise Miller, is the daughter
of an honest musician, and has given her heart to
Ferdinand von Walter, the son of one who holds the
highest position in the principality next to the sovereign
—that of President of the Council. Ferdinand is a
youth of an ardent, generous, and romantic nature, and
is fully resolved to make Luise his wife. Her mother
is proud of her good fortune; but her father feels that
the relation can lead only to disaster, and insists that
Luise shall abandon her aristocratic lover and accept a
husband of her own station. Ferdinand's father, the
President, assumes that the young man is only amusing
himself, and makes arrangements for a marriage between
him and Lady Milford, an Englishwoman, (of the house
of Norfolk!) who has been for some time the prince's
mistress. Lady Milford loves Ferdinand, and fervently
hopes that he will assent to his father's plan. To her
surprise, and still more to that of the President, Ferdinand firmly rejects her offered hand, and announces his
intention of marrying, at whatever sacrifice, the musician's daughter. The President, having convinced himself that he cannot achieve his design by force, has
recourse to stratagem. He orders the arrest of Luise's
father and mother; and then, filled with horror at what
seems to be their impending fate, she is induced to write
a letter to a person who has been paying court to her,
making an appointment with him, and pretending that
she has never loved Ferdinand. This letter is conveyed
to her lover, whose heart is broken by so terrible a reve-

lation. He gathers himself together for a last act of
revenge, and discovers the truth only when the poison,
which he himself has drunk and which he has given
to Luise, has taken effect, and they are both in their
death-agonies.

So violent a conclusion leaves us dissatisfied, unless
we feel that it is absolutely inevitable, and it cannot be
said that Schiller convinces us of its necessity. A word
from Luise would at once enlighten Ferdinand, and there
is no sufficient reason why the word should not be spoken
in their final interview. Indeed, the device by which
he is deceived is so gross, that he almost forfeits our
sympathy for not immediately perceiving its real character, or at any rate for not suspecting treachery. It is
a striking testimony to the genius of the play that this
scarcely diminishes the interest of the spectators at the
moment of representation; they are too swiftly borne
along by the torrent of emotion to be fully conscious of
weakness and inconsistency in the conduct either of the
hero or the heroine. No single figure in "Intrigue and
Love" is so striking as Karl Moor; on the other hand,
all are more truly conceived than Franz Moor, the elder
Moor, and Amalia. Both Luise and Ferdinand, although
they protest too much, and in too sentimental a tone,
are admirable types of passion breaking itself against the
barriers of social convention; and in Miller there is a
most lifelike presentment of an irascible, but honest and
kind, father. The ardour of the lovers has a perfect foil
in the coldness, selfishness, and cruelty of the President;
and although the Court-Marshal, to whom Luise is made
to address her fatal letter, seems now to be a figure only
suited for burlesque, his utmost follies were not incredible

to Schiller's contemporaries. In some respects all these characters are surpassed by Lady Milford, who, notwithstanding her degradation, cherishes tender memories and a lingering faith in purity. There is both strength and delicacy in the art with which her better nature is made to awake through the loyal affection of the lovers, whom she in vain attempts to separate.

The poems written by Schiller during the early part of his career, so far as their substance is concerned, have essentially the same character as his dramas. They are the passionate outpourings of a mind which has become conscious of its capacities, but has not learned either to look at the world steadily or to control its own sympathies and yearnings. The most ambitious of these efforts is a satirical and didactic poem, "The Chariot of Venus" ("Der Venuswagen"), issued separately soon after the publication of "The Robbers." It is intended to display the ruin caused by unbridled passion, and there is hardly a stanza which is not marked by energy of expression and freedom of movement. The effect of the whole, however, is marred by too bold a handling of matters, about which the wisest are, perhaps, those who feel most inclined to be silent. Several other poems of this period manifest the same audacity without the excuse of a didactic motive. Yet, in "The Triumph of Love" ("Der Triumph der Liebe"), Schiller's point of view is so exalted that love appears as a sentiment adapted only to natures of angelic refinement. In these early lyrics he seems to know no middle way between idealism without passion, and passion without idealism; and the consequence, of course, is, that neither his idealism nor his passion has the charm of true poetry. The images in the Odes to Laura are so indefinite that they tell us nothing of the qualities which excite his enthusiasm, and the poet appears to be more interested in the vague philosophic fancies suggested by his relation to Laura than in Laura herself.   A truer chord is touched in his Ode on "Friendship" ("Die Freundschaft"), in which he writes with the warmth of experience.   In this powerful poem, which is remarkable for the pomp and splendour of its language, Schiller generalises the attraction between kindred minds until it becomes the type of the forces that give coherence and unity to the Cosmos. His political poems, "The Conqueror" ("Der Eroberer") and "The Bad Monarchs" ("Die Schlimmen Monarchen"), contain little more than a vehement protest, extravagant in form if not in feeling, against tyranny. "Flowers" ("Die Blumen"), and the lines "To Spring" ("An den Frühling"), are the expression of a sincere delight in nature, but give no evidence of exact and fine observation.   One of the best of these early writings is a poem on Rousseau, in which he celebrates with enthusiasm the virtues of the master by whom he had been so much influenced, and contrasts his free spirit with the narrowness and prejudice of his age.   In "Count Eberhard," Schiller records a pathetic incident in the history of Würtemberg, and it is interesting as the first indication in his minor poems of the vivid force and directness of his later ballads.

CHAPTER VI.

IN DRESDEN AND WEIMAR.

WHEN Schiller reached Leipsic (on the 17th of April 1785), his friend Körner was in Dresden, where he held the office of Councillor to the Supreme Consistorial Court. Schiller was, however, warmly welcomed by the sisters, Minna and Dora Stock, and by Huber, a youth of an affectionate and enthusiastic temperament, but without any distinguished intellectual qualities. The spring fair was in progress at the time of Schiller's arrival, and he heartily enjoyed the stir and movement which give the streets of Leipsic a gay and animated appearance on these occasions. The booksellers gladly did honour to a poet from whom such great things were expected, and he found that literary men of every grade of merit and pretension were pleased to make his acquaintance.

Soon after his arrival in Leipsic, Schiller began to review his position seriously; and as he did so, the image of Margareta Schwan rose more and more clearly before him. Now that he was free from the influence of Frau von Kalb, his love for Margareta revived; and he felt sure that, if he could win her, she would give unity

and charm to his life. He accordingly wrote to Schwan,
begging that he might have permission to ask her to become his wife. Schiller was obliged to confess that he
could not for some time offer her a home; but he had
resolved, he said, to devote himself again to the medical
profession, and he did not doubt that he would soon
have a sufficient practice. He had always received so
much kindness from Schwan, and Margareta and he had
bidden each other so affectionate a farewell (promising
to be faithful correspondents), that he looked forward
with confidence to the reply. Schwan, however, was
not attracted by the proposal, and promptly answered
that he did not think the character of his daughter
would accord well with that of Schiller. So vanished
another dream; and in the end Schiller had good reason
to congratulate himself that his wish had not been gratified. He continued for some time afterwards to think
of practising as a physician, but the idea was by-and-by
finally abandoned.

Wishing to have leisure and quiet for literary work,
he hired a room in Gohlis, a pretty village in the Rosen-
thal, within easy walking distance of Leipsic, and here
he spent the summer of 1785. That he had many happy
hours during this summer may be assumed, if (as is most
probable) the verses "To Joy" ("An die Freude")
were written in Gohlis. In Mannheim he had worked
from time to time at "Don Carlos," and now he occupied
himself with it still more seriously; he also gave many
hours to 'Thalia,' although without hope of being able
to issue it as frequently as he had originally intended.
On the 1st of July he met Körner for the first time, and
each immediately recognised in the other a friend to

whom he might give his whole heart. Soon afterwards, Körner not only delivered Schiller again from a temporary difficulty, but asked to be permitted to provide for him during the following year.

In August 1785, Körner and Minna Stock were married, and they immediately established themselves in Dresden, taking with them Minna's sister Dora. About a month afterwards they were joined by Schiller, and for nearly two years he was virtually an inmate of their house. The first weeks were spent at Loschwitz, a village on the Elbe near Dresden, where Körner possessed a vineyard with a summer-house, commanding a lovely view of the distant mountains of Saxon Switzerland. As winter approached they returned to Dresden, and Schiller took up his abode in rooms which had been hired for him opposite Körner's dwelling. These rooms were in a short time shared by Huber, who had entered the diplomatic career, and had received his first appointment at the Saxon Court. The morning was given by Schiller to work ; he then joined the Körners at dinner, and spent with them the afternoon and evening. Sometimes they had visitors, but they generally preferred to be alone ; and a charming little society they formed, marked by perfect freedom and refinement. The experience of these months left a deep impression on Schiller's mind and character. Melancholy enough he often felt, for his future was still dark, but he was cheered and strengthened by constant association with friends who appreciated his genius and loved him for his own sake. And in several directions his intellectual life was deepened and widened by Körner's influence. Körner was an ardent student of Kant; and although he

could not at this time induce Schiller to join him in
his studies, he often made philosophy the subject of
their conversation. Partly owing to Körner, too, Schiller began to give much attention to history.

Excellent as Schiller's opportunities now were, the
only important work which he completed during his
residence in Dresden was "Don Carlos." It gave him
far more trouble than he had anticipated, the expansion
of his plan making it necessary for him to introduce numerous changes. In May 1787, however, it was finished ;
and although there was a remarkable diversity of critical
opinion as to its merits, the first edition was quickly
exhausted, and in some theatres it was brilliantly suc-
cessful. For a long time he was known chiefly as the
author of "The Robbers" and "Don Carlos," and the
latter may be said to have made his fame secure. Three
numbers of 'Thalia' were published, and he had no
reason to be dissatisfied either with the manner in which
they were received by the public or paid by the bookseller. The first number (issued in Mannheim) had contained the first act of "Don Carlos ;" the second and
third acts were included in subsequent numbers. In
these numbers appeared also the "Philosophical Letters"
("Philosophische Briefe"), and a part of "The Visionary" ("Der Geisterseher").

Early in 1787 Schiller went with the Körners to a
masked ball, and was addressed by a graceful and frolic-
some damsel who at once made a "conquest" of him.
She proved to be Henriette von Arnim, a charming girl
of about nineteen, the daughter of a widow who held the
position of *gouvernante* of the ladies of the Dresden
Court. Frau von Arnim was not inclined to give her

daughter to a poor poet, however famous; but she did not
altogether discourage him, as there was a chance that his
devotion would stimulate the ardour of more "eligible"
lovers. The young lady herself, although by no means
indifferent to the advantages of wealth and high birth,
seems to have loved Schiller sincerely; and he was soon
completely mastered by his passion. The Körners liked
neither her nor her family, and did what they could to
break the connection, but in vain. Work became impossible, and of his small earnings a considerable part
was spent in pretty presents for Henriette and her
mother. At Easter he was persuaded to take a short
holiday at the little town of Tharand, but here he
thought more than ever of his new love, and at last he
wrote to Henriette, telling her how necessary she had
become to his happiness. The letter which he received
in reply was as passionate as his own; yet there was
something in its tone which displeased him, and on his
return to Dresden she found that he no longer wished
her to be more than his friend. The change did not
break her heart, but her romance was perhaps deeper
than Schiller suspected, for during her future life (and
her life was a very checkered one) his portrait always
hung in her room.

After the completion of "Don Carlos," Schiller began
to feel that he must make another effort to test the possibilities of fortune. His love for Körner was unabated,
but his intellectual life needed a fresh impulse, and it
had become manifest that he could not hope to find in
Dresden a settled position. More than thirty years
before, when in much the same kind of perplexity,
Lessing had turned naturally to Berlin, which then took

the lead in German literature; but its influence had since passed to Weimar, where a brilliant Court had been able to attract Wieland, Goethe, and Herder. Almost every young man of letters hoped that, like these great writers, he might find a patron in the generous Duke; and many a pilgrimage was made to the little capital with vague expectations, which could not, of course, be realised. Schiller, however, was justified in looking to Weimar for help, for already he was in the foremost rank of contemporary poets, and by making him a Councillor the Duke had given him signal proof of goodwill. To Weimar, therefore, he resolved to go; and on the 20th of July 1787 he started on his journey, having spent the previous evening with his friends at Loschwitz, recalling the happy days they had enjoyed together, and making many promises of continued attachment. And the promises were kept. To the end of his life it was one of his deepest pleasures to open his heart to Körner, from whom he had received so many evidences of solid judgment and warm sympathy; and their delightful correspondence throws a vivid light on the changes of thought and feeling which found gradual expression in Schiller's greatest writings.

For some time Frau von Kalb had been in Weimar, and she was the first to welcome him to this new scene. Her love for him was unaltered; and in her presence he seemed to be attracted to her by as strong a fascination as ever. She was in delicate health, being threatened with total blindness, and had gone to Weimar for the purpose of being attended by a famous oculist. This gave her a fresh claim to Schiller's sympathy; and she was delighted to have the opportunity of introducing

him to the society of Weimar, where she was well
known and much liked. "Charlotte," he wrote to
Körner, "is a great strange mind—a real study for me.
At every step in our intercourse I discover new qualities
in her, which surprise and enchant me like beautiful
scenes in a wide landscape." He was about, however,
to form many new relations; and by-and-by he was glad
to break off an intimacy which had excited and disturbed him without giving him an hour of genuine
happiness.

The Duke had gone to Potsdam, and remained away
for many months; and Goethe was in Italy, from which
he did not return until the following year. Schiller,
therefore, found no trace of that varied and brilliant life
which had made Weimar famous for several years.
There was still, however, much to interest him, and he
lost no time in making himself known to those who
were likely to care for his acquaintance. His first visit
was to Wieland, who had pleased him by acknowledg-
ing the genius of "The Robbers," although frankly criti-
cising its extravagance. Wieland was now fifty-four
years of age; and although he had still many years of
labour before him, he had done all the work by which
his name lives. One of his chief occupations was the
editing of 'Mercury,' a periodical by which he exerted
considerable influence on the movements of literary
opinion. In his intercourse with men he had all the
humours and fancies of a child, taking offence for no
apparent reason, and becoming friendly again by a sudden impulse; but when he was in the mood nobody
could be more agreeable. He spent two hours with
Schiller in pleasant talk; and afterwards, when Schiller

thoroughly understood his light and wayward temper, they became good friends, and were able to work together harmoniously for ' Mercury.' Herder was visited next, and Schiller felt powerfully attracted by his grave and noble spirit. Schiller's writings were known to Herder only by reputation, but he was prepared to think favourably of them, and he liked the writer himself so well that he repeatedly expressed a wish that they might meet often. Much of their conversation was about Goethe, whom, as Schiller told Körner, Herder loved "with passion, with a kind of idolatry."

The attractions of the society of Weimar were not favourable to work ; but Schiller was soon reminded of the necessity of resisting them by the rapid diminution of his supply of money, which he had been obliged to borrow, on Körner's security, before leaving Dresden. Poetry and the drama had hitherto been so unprofitable, that it occurred to him to try whether he might not turn to advantage his recent historical studies.   In writing "Don Carlos" he had become familiar with the age of Philip II., and he now determined to make one particular phase of it—the revolt of the Netherlands—the subject of an elaborate work. He had no sooner formed this resolution than he collected his authorities, began to study them in earnest, and drew the outlines of his plan. He now went seldom into society, and was generally at his desk ten or twelve hours daily. "I am full of my materials," he assured Körner, "and work with pleasure. It is my *début* in history, and I hope to produce something that will be very readable."

In November 1787, he received from Frau von Wolzogen an urgent request to visit her at Bauerbach. Since they last met she had been in serious difficulties, and had been forced to make repeated applications to Schiller for the repayment of the money she had lent him. He had not been able to discharge any part of his debt, but this had not interrupted their friendship; and she was now particularly anxious to see him, as she wished to have his opinion of the man whom her daughter was about to marry. He willingly accepted her invitation, and spent a pleasant fortnight, partly in Bauerbach, partly in Meiningen, where his sister Christophine was now settled as Frau Reinwald.

On the way back to Weimar he was accompanied by his old fellow-student, Wilhelm von Wolzogen. They travelled on horseback, and on a gloomy December evening rode together into Rudolstadt. As they passed a pretty house, standing apart in the midst of a large garden, Wilhelm looked up and saw two handsome young women watching them from a window. They were his cousins, the daughters of Frau von Lengefeld, and he laughingly hid his face in his mantle. Schiller rode gravely on, but not without exciting the curiosity of his companion's friends. Soon afterwards Wilhelm called and asked permission to return with Schiller.

This was a memorable evening to Schiller, for it was now that he met the lady who, about two years afterwards, became his wife. Frau von Lengefeld, a mild and kindly gentlewoman, was the widow of a man of good birth and superior intelligence, who had made a considerable reputation by his extensive knowledge of all matters relating to forests. After his death, about ten years before this time, she continued to live in Rudolstadt with her two daughters; and the elder daughter,

Caroline, married in early youth a Herr von Beulwitz, who took up his residence in the house of his mother-in-law. He was generally respected, but the marriage was not a happy one; ultimately it was dissolved, and Caroline married Wilhelm von Wolzogen, to whom she was already warmly attached. Her sister Charlotte, about three years younger, was now twenty-one; and although she was not remarkably beautiful, she had, according to Caroline, "a very agreeable figure and face." "An expression of the purest goodness of heart," says Caroline, "animated her features; and her eyes, which were blue, flashed only truth and innocence. Thoughtful, and sensitive to everything good and beautiful in life and in art, her whole nature had a beautiful harmony." She had a talent for drawing, and occasionally wrote verses, which in Caroline's opinion were "full of grace and gentle feeling." In childhood the sisters had been carefully trained by their father, and one result of his teaching was that they shared his enthusiastic admiration for Frederick the Great, who had invited him to settle in Prussia. Occasionally they saw something of "the great world;" for their family was highly respected by the Duke of Weimar and other princes. All the famous writers of Weimar they knew; and Goethe had sometimes been their guest. Much of their time they spent in reading—their favourite author being Plutarch, to whom they returned again and again; but this did not prevent them from appreciating the literature of their own period and country. In their quiet home they had thus an ideal world of their own; and "often," says Caroline, "we seemed to ourselves to be enchanted princesses, waiting for our deliverer."

In such a circle, so full of life and intelligence, Schiller could not but be happy. Long before, in Mannheim, he had seen Frau von Lengefeld and her daughters for a few minutes on their way back from Switzerland; but he was then ill and depressed, and the meeting had made no impression on him. Now he felt the full charm of these bright and ardent natures, with their fine aptitudes, generous enthusiasms, and delicate sympathies. They knew his early writings, and expressed pleasure at the prospect of reading "Don Carlos," which he promised to send to them. So agreeably did the evening pass, that in saying good-bye Schiller declared he would probably return to Rudolstadt in the following spring, and work there during summer—a scheme which was warmly encouraged by his new friends.

Schiller returned to Weimar with a deep affection for Caroline; but for Lotte he had conceived a passionate love, which immediately gave a new aim and direction to his energies. From this time she was never far from his thoughts, and he cherished an eager hope that the light which burned steadily in his own heart would soon burn as steadily in hers. As he could not venture to express his hope until he had some definite prospect of being able to form a home, he began to work with more ardour than he had ever before manifested. His history of the revolt of the Netherlands made rapid progress, and among other labours he returned to "The Visionary," although with a growing repugnance to the story, as he saw how difficult it would be to bring it to a satisfactory close.

He soon had an opportunity of developing his relation to Lotte, who came to visit a friend in Weimar, partly

that the Duchess might be reminded of a promise to
provide her with a position at Court. At this time they
did not often meet; but Lotte saw enough of him to
make her rank him among her most intimate friends, and
she received from him several letters, between the lines
of which it is easy to read his secret. On one occasion
she invited him to spend the following evening at the
house in which she was living, if there was no particular
attraction at the play. "I could almost be provoked,"
he replied, "that the play is not better, or that there is
not some greater pleasure, that I might be able to show
you how gladly I give it up for the happiness of being
near you." The letter ends: "As I wrote, a passing
sledge drew me to the window; and it was you! I
have seen you, and that is at any rate something for
to-day." In a note written immediately before her
return to Rudolstadt, she spoke of the pleasure which
she had found in his "companionship," adding, paren-
thetically, "I must not say friendship, since you do
not like the word." "You really believe," he answered,
"that I object to the word friendship? After what
I may have said of the misuse of the term, I might
perhaps seem too proud if I claimed to be your friend;
but the name shall not disturb me. Let the grain of
seed shoot up: when the spring sun shines on it, we
shall see what flower will come of it."

The parting was made easy to Schiller by the hope
that he would soon be near her again; for he had decided to spend the summer of 1788 in Rudolstadt, and
Lotte undertook to find a lodging for him. After much
looking about, she hired rooms in a quiet village, Volkstädt, near Rudolstadt. "The village," she wrote, "has

a beautiful position on the bank of the Saale. Behind
are hills crowned with dark wood, while all around are
fruitful fields ; on the opposite side of the river there is
a view of beautiful meadows, and of a wide, long valley." On one of the hills there is now a bronze copy of
Dannecker's splendid bust of Schiller ; and no neighbourhood could be more appropriately associated with
his name, for here, if anywhere, he was happy. Having
worked all day in his room, he generally walked, late in
the afternoon, towards Rudolstadt, following the wind-
ings of the Saale by a path which skirted corn-fields and
orchards ; and on a bridge that spanned a tiny brook,
he often found the two lovely sisters waiting for him.
"How happy we were," says Caroline, "when after a
tiresome afternoon visit we were able to go to meet our
genial friend under the beautiful trees on the banks of the
Saale ! When we saw his figure against the glow of the
evening sky, a joyful, ideal life opened before us. In
conversation with Schiller, we seemed to wander alternately among the flowers of the earth and the immutable
stars of heaven." Often as he now saw Lotte, messengers frequently passed between the two houses with
letters ; and Schiller said so much, that it is surprising
he did not take courage to say more. "Again," he wrote
in one letter, "the evening vanished so quickly ! Often
I have so much to say to you, and when I leave, I find
that I have said nothing. When I am near you, I feel
only that it is well with me, and I enjoy my happiness
in silence too much to be able to give it utterance."
When the days shortened, and the nights became chilly,
he shifted his quarters from Volkstädt to Rudolstadt.
He then saw Lotte even more frequently; but they still

wrote to one another, and each successive letter, playful in form, but with a touch of seriousness, seemed to bring them nearer to the goal.

The evenings were not altogether spent in talk : Schiller read with his friends Voss's translation of the Odyssey, and a prose translation of the Iliad. Fascinated by Homer, he began also to study the Greek dramatists, learning for the first time to appreciate classic purity and grace. The sisters begged him to give them a poetical rendering of some of the passages he admired; and thus stimulated, he gradually translated the "Iphigenia in Aulis," and parts of the "Phœnissæ," of Euripides, afterwards publishing his translations in 'Thalia.' "This work," he wrote to Körner, "exercises me in dramatic writing, enables me to understand the spirit of the Greeks, and, unconsciously to myself, gives me, I hope, their manner."

His happiness was sadly interrupted by tidings of the sudden death of Frau von Wolzogen, in whom he had found so faithful a friend. She died on the 5th of August, and a few days afterwards Wilhelm von Wolzogen received a letter, in which Schiller declared that "the recollection of her would live eternally in his soul." "All the love," he continued, "which my heart devoted to her, I will cherish for her son, and regard it as a debt which I owe her in her grave. We must belong to each other as brothers. Ah! she was to me everything that a mother could have been."

An incident, which Schiller never forgot, marked the summer of 1788—his first meeting with Goethe. It took place in Frau von Lengefeld's house; and the sisters had looked forward to the event with the greatest

interest, for they did not doubt that Goethe and Schiller
would be at once attracted to each other. They were,
however, disappointed. Goethe was polite to Schiller,
—no more; and Schiller made no attempt to conciliate
him. "On the whole," he wrote to Körner, "my great
idea of Goethe has not been diminished by personal
acquaintance; but I doubt whether we shall ever approach each other nearly. Much that is still interesting to me, and that I have to wish and hope for,
is no longer of importance to him. He is so far ahead
of me, less in years than in experience of life and in
self-development, that we shall never meet on our separate paths. His whole nature is constituted otherwise
than mine; his world is not mine; our modes of
thought appear to be essentially different. A final judgment, however, cannot be formed from such a meeting;
time will reveal the rest."

Schiller spent in Rudolstadt his twenty-ninth birth-
day; and on the evening of the 12th of November he
was once more in Weimar. The decisive word had not
been spoken to Lotte; but his unalterable resolve was to
make for himself a career which would justify him in
asking her to share his fortunes. He no sooner returned
to Weimar than he formed many new plans; and he
worked so hard that his friends expostulated with him
on the injury which he would almost certainly inflict on
his health. One of his schemes was to make Frederick
the Great the hero of an epic poem. The idea had been
suggested by Körner, and had at once attracted Schiller.
He decided to select a period in which Frederick had
displayed undaunted courage in adversity; but the poem
was to represent the whole spirit and progress of the eigh-

teenth century. Ultimately he abandoned this intention, but not without regret. Had it been accomplished, perhaps fewer critics would have been of opinion that the thirteen years devoted to Frederick by the foremost English man of letters of the present age were altogether misspent.

Meanwhile, Schiller's history of the revolt of the Netherlands, part of which had been published in Wieland's 'Mercury,' was finished; and its appearance was destined to have a far more important influence on his course than he anticipated. It occurred to a friend of his, Voigt, that the services of one who could write so well on history ought, if possible, to be secured for the neighbouring university of Jena. The idea was communicated to Goethe; and as there happened to be a vacancy in the staff of professors, he entered into it heartily. Schiller was "sounded," and hesitated whether it would be worth his while to sanction the scheme. Then, as now, there were two classes of professors in German universities — full professors and professors extraordinary. It was proposed that Schiller should belong to the second class, without any fixed salary. After much consideration, he announced that if he were offered the appointment he would accept it. The University of Jena being the common property of the Saxon Duchies, the matter could not be formally settled at once; but, on the 15th December, he informed Körner that Goethe had sent him a rescript, indicating that, since the Government of Weimar was satisfied, no objection would be made by the other Governments, and that he might safely begin his preparations for his new duties.

Although Goethe played so kindly a part in this

matter, he had manifested no inclination to cultivate the acquaintance of Schiller. As he himself explains in "Wahrheit und Dichtung," he had returned from Italy with a very different conception of the aims and methods of poetry from that with which he had opened his career. His study of classical literature, and of the masterpieces of ancient art, had shown him that it is not enough to have the impulses of genius, and that literature falls short of perfection in so far as it is deficient in order, measure, and calm. Schiller himself was gradually approaching a kindred view; but this was unknown to Goethe. The work with which he mainly connected Schiller was "The Robbers," and it displayed only restless, ungovernable passion. He had therefore a prejudice against the author, and held aloof from him, resisting the efforts of common friends to bring them together. Schiller was too proud to intrude on any one; yet he was always thinking of Goethe, and could hardly write a letter without bringing in an allusion to him. "Goethe excites in me," he wrote, "a quite peculiar mixture of hatred and love, a feeling not unlike that which Brutus and Cassius must have had towards Cæsar. I could destroy his spirit, and yet heartily love him again." For the most part, the balance seems not to have inclined to love; and the fact, it is to be feared, was hardly due to disinterested observation. "Once for all," he wrote to Körner, "this man, this Goethe, is in my way; and he often reminds me of the hard manner in which I have been treated by fate. How lightly was *his* genius borne by his destiny, and how have I been compelled to struggle even to the present moment!" Caroline, who intensely admired both poets, was vexed that they did not understand each other; and she tried earnestly to modify Schiller's opinion of his rival. This was the response to her efforts: " If Goethe is really so very amiable, I shall find it out, no doubt, in that world where we shall all be angels. Seriously, I am too indolent and too proud to wait upon a man until he unfolds himself before me. There is a saying which all men understand; it is, Exercise your powers ! Any one who works with his whole energy cannot be concealed from others. That is *my* plan."

When this was written, Schiller had urgent need to " exercise his powers." He had now a heavy burden of debt, and in order to deliver himself from some part of it, as well as to provide his daily bread, he was obliged to devote himself to many uncongenial tasks. At the same time, as he had not a profound knowledge of history, he could not avoid the necessity of preparing for his approaching lectures by extensive reading. Thus the days passed in incessant labour and anxiety—with, however, a gleam of happier possibilities when he received his weekly letter from Lotte—until the 11th of May 1789. On that day he left Weimar, and took possession of his new abode in Jena.

86

CHAPTER VII.

"DON CARLOS," AND SOME LYRICS.

THE Don Carlos of history was born in 1545. He was
masterful and wayward, but essentially generous, and
endowed with considerable intellectual gifts. During
boyhood his impulses were subject to no control, his
mother having died at his birth, and his father, Philip
II., being absent in the Netherlands and in England.
On the return of Philip to Madrid in 1559 he soon
alienated the affections of his son by harsh treatment;
and the repugnance which they felt for each other
became so bitter, that in 1567, dreading treachery, Don
Carlos resolved to fly from Spain. This came to the
knowledge of the gloomy king, who immediately caused
him to be arrested, and submitted his case to the investigation of a mock tribunal. He was reported to be
insane, and a few months afterwards died. His death
was attributed to natural causes; but it is probable
that he was either poisoned or driven by despair to take
his own life.

This strange history was brought to the notice of
Schiller by Dalberg, the director of the Mannheim
theatre, and, like other dramatists who have dealt with

it, he immediately recognised its fitness for tragedy. At this time he was still dominated by the temper which marks his first three dramas, and he was attracted to the new subject partly by the opportunities which the horrors of the Inquisition would offer for the same kind of writing. In other respects the drama, as he wrote to Dalberg, was to be "a family picture in a royal house,— the situation of a father who is the unhappy rival of his son, of a son who loves without hope and is sacrificed." The third wife of Philip II. was the Princess Elizabeth, daughter of Henry II. of France. It had been proposed that she should become the wife of Don Carlos; and Schiller drew the tragic motive of his play from the fiction (invented by St Réal, from whose historical romance he obtained most of his materials) that the prince had passionately loved her, and continued to love her after her marriage with his father. At an early stage in the play Don Carlos reveals the energy of his passion in an interview with the queen in the garden of her country-house at Aranjuez. This interview is arranged by his friend, the Marquis Posa, who does not yet understand the real nature of his feelings. For some time Posa plays a subordinate part; but he is from the beginning represented as a man of a noble and disinterested ambition, and through him Don Carlos is inspired with a longing for a position in which he may be able to forget his sorrows in the fulfilment of great duties. The Netherlands are in revolt, and Don Carlos asks to be sent thither at the head of an army, entreating the king, in a scene of remarkable power, not to exclude his son any longer from his affection and confidence. The task of subduing the Netherlands is intrusted (as in history) to Alva, but Philip has been touched by the appeal to his sympathies, and determines to associate Don Carlos with him in the government. Meanwhile a page hands to the prince a letter in which a lady who does not sign her name declares her love for him, inclosing a key to a certain cabinet in the queen's pavilion. He assumes that the queen is the writer, and immediately all his good resolutions are abandoned. But the lady whom he finds in the cabinet is the Princess Eboli, who to her dismay quickly discovers that she has misunderstood him, and that he loves some one else. She penetrates to his secret, and, enraged by disappointment and jealousy, arouses the suspicions of the king. Philip's mood is still further darkened by his confessor Domingo, and by Alva, both of whom hate Don Carlos, and unite in suggesting a doubt as to the queen's honour. Their charges are fiercely resented; but in reality Philip knows not what to think or how to act, and he bitterly deplores that he has not a single counsellor to whom he can look for help. Glancing through a list of persons who have done him service, he comes upon the name of the Marquis Posa, twice underlined; and on inquiry he receives such enthusiastic reports of Posa's character, that Alva is directed to bring him without delay to the royal cabinet.

The circumstances of Schiller's life prevented him from reaching this point in the play for several years; and during that time a great change had passed over his modes of thought and feeling. In the first period of his career, hatred of despotism and convention so possessed his nature that he was hardly conscious of the sense of humanity from which it sprang; but in Dresden, surrounded by sympathetic friends, the sense of

humanity became his dominant feeling. This was the
characteristic sentiment of all the noblest minds of the
eighteenth century ; and in no mind had it deeper roots
than in that of Schiller. He longed with almost passionate ardour for the happiness of mankind ; and with
this growing feeling he now associated positive convic-
tions respecting the true order of the world. The merely
destructive impulse had spent itself ; he thought rather
of the establishment of new forms of society than of
the process by which the old forms were to be removed.
His enthusiasm was, if possible, stronger than before ;
but it was an enthusiasm, not for revolution, but for re-
construction.   It was too late to make Don Carlos, de-
voured by an unhappy passion, the representative of his
altered mood ; accordingly he gave new importance to
the Marquis Posa, who from this time becomes the central figure of the tragedy.   No thought of his own advantage crosses Posa's mind : he is absorbed by love for his
friend, by love for the world ; and he is entranced by
the vision of a fair social life which, as he believes, will
one day emerge from the misapprehensions and confu-
sions by which man is now separated from man, and
nation from nation.

Introduced into the king's cabinet, Posa sets forth the
grievances of the Netherlands, and depicts with fervent
eloquence the glory which Philip might achieve by
granting just institutions. The selfish heart of the old
monarch is for an instant moved, and he makes Posa his
first Minister, intrusting to him the duty of finding out
the truth respecting his wife and his son. Unfortunately the measures adopted by Posa are misunderstood
by Don Carlos, who, fancying that he is being betrayed,

goes to the Princess Eboli and implores her to permit
him to speak with the queen. Posa interrupts them,
and fears that all is lost. His first impulse is to kill the
Princess Eboli, but as he points his dagger at her breast,
a sudden thought suggests itself—he may, perhaps, be
able to save the prince by sacrificing himself. He writes
a letter addressed to the Prince of Orange, pretending that
he loves the queen, and saying that Don Carlos has
visited the Princess Eboli, evidently with the intention
of putting the king on his guard. He intends, therefore,
he declares, to escape from Madrid and join the rebels.
Posa takes care that this letter shall fall into Philip's
hands. Meanwhile he has made it impossible for Don
Carlos to commit any further indiscretion, by causing
him to be arrested; and having said farewell to the
queen, he visits the prince and narrates what he has
done, showing that he has been impelled not only by
affection, but by the hope that his friend will henceforth
use his powers only for great and unselfish ends. As
they converse, a shot is fired between the bars of the
cell, and Posa falls. The king and his courtiers enter;
and Don Carlos, over Posa's body, tells the story of his
self-sacrifice, and vows eternal enmity to his murderer.
Aroused by Posa's heroism, Don Carlos feels himself
delivered from his passion, devotes himself to the cause
of liberty, and determines to proceed without delay to
the Netherlands. At midnight, however, he contrives
to see the queen, and they are saying a few last words
when the king and the Grand Inquisitor suddenly appear before them. The queen faints; and Philip, turning to the Grand Inquisitor, says coldly and calmly,
" Cardinal, I have done my duty; do yours."

The grand defect of "Don Carlos" is that it lacks unity of design. Throughout the first part of the play the interest is centred in the prince; throughout the remainder, except in the concluding scenes, he is almost passive, and attention is absorbed by the ideal figure of the Marquis Posa. The elements of the tragedy are not, therefore, combined in a coherent scheme, and the total impression is disturbed and confused. In several scenes there are strange inconsistencies of feeling and conduct. Had Don Carlos seen that the letter addressed to him by the Princess Eboli could not have been written by the queen, the action must have taken a wholly different course. His misapprehension is attributed to the fact that he does not know the queen's handwriting; yet soon afterwards it is shown that he had at one time corresponded with her, and that he always carries one of her letters in his bosom. Apart, however, from this, the spectator is shocked by the readiness with which Don Carlos believes that such a letter can have come from a lady whose honour and purity are beyond reproach. The most splendid eloquence fails to withdraw attention from such faults as these: nevertheless, "Don Carlos" stands on a much higher level than Schiller's early dramas. In the first place, it is in verse; and he already displays an astonishing mastery of the iambic measure, especially when he uses it for the purpose of giving voice to lofty thoughts and aspirations. And the characters are, as a rule, more finely conceived than any of those we have hitherto met. A deeply pathetic impression is produced by the queen, whose patience and resignation suggest a world of passionate feeling suppressed by circumstances. The Princess Eboli, too, is a

lifelike study, equally natural in her love, her jealousy,
her degradation, and her repentance. The world asso-
ciates the name of Alva with so tragic a conflict in real
life, that we dislike to see him, as in "Don Carlos," play
the part of an intriguing courtier; and Domingo and the
Grand Inquisitor are rather caricatures than types of
their class, since it is incredible that even the Inquisition
had no other origin than a coarse thirst for power. On
the other hand, springs of true feeling are touched in
Lerma, a courtier, who from time to time, at considerable risk, warns Don Carlos of his peril. The nature of
the passion which governs Don Carlos prevents him
from becoming an object of complete sympathy until he
rises above it; but the resources of Schiller's art are
grandly displayed in the means by which we are constantly reminded of the worthier impulses that contend
for mastery in the prince's deep and agitated spirit.
The figure, however, which gives an enduring charm to
this great although imperfect drama, is the Marquis
Posa. In him the eighteenth century found the highest
expression of some of its most splendid characteristics,
—its faith in man, its longing for an age in which the individual shall be free and yet feel bound to his fellows
by the ties of inward charity. The Marquis Posa is a
living proof that, before the French Revolution began,
the battle between the dying and the coming era had
already been virtually fought out. It has been often
objected that there is something unnatural and incredible
in the sudden resolve of Philip to make Posa his first
Minister; and it may be admitted that the real Philip,
hard, narrow, and selfish, would have been incapable of
so romantic a stroke. But, as his character is conceived

by Schiller, his conduct hardly surprises us.   Here he is
not a mere sombre tyrant : he is accessible to emotion ;
he feels his loneliness, and craves for the support of a
strong and generous nature.   In the ideal world of the
drama, it seems almost a matter of course that a king of
this temper should succumb to Posa's authority ; for
Posa has more than simple goodness,—he has the radiance
and the fascination of genius : we feel, in his glowing
words, the stirring of mysterious forces which must
transform the face of society.   The devices by which he
attempts to secure the deliverance of Don Carlos are not
happily conceived ; but we scarcely observe their forced
and artificial character, so potent is the attraction of the
friendship and humanity which shine through them, and
which at last rob death itself of its terrors.   When the
conflict which rages in the breast of Don Carlos is ended
by the triumph of his good genius, we are impressed by
the conviction that it could have had no other issue,
since worthy energies could not but be evoked in one
for whom so great a life had sacrificed itself.   Criticism
in vain attempts to obscure this genial creation : it has
never lost its interest for Schiller's countrymen ; and for
the young especially, the Marquis Posa shines as the
morning star of German freedom.

During these years Schiller worked occasionally at
another play, which was to bear the title of "The
Misanthrope" ("Der Menschenfeind"). His intention
apparently was to depict the process by which a man of
soured disposition is reconciled to humanity ; but the
subject was not congenial, and the work remained a
fragment.   Of more importance than this broken scheme
are the poems produced in Schiller's second period.

They are few in number, but indicate a remarkable advance both in range of feeling and in mastery of poetic diction. The hymn "To Joy" is a record of one of those moments in which the mind rises above the limits of ordinary life, and breathes the atmosphere of a calm and flawless world. At such times Schiller was always impelled to generalise his emotions; and here, with overflowing gladness in his own heart, he sees in joy (as he had formerly seen in friendship) the hidden spring which moves the powers of the universe. "The Gods of Greece" ("Die Götter Griechenlands") was written in response to a demand for an immediate contribution to 'Mercury,' but there is no trace of hurry in its majestic images. It presents a powerful contrast between the unimaginative conceptions of modern times and the spirit which led the Greeks to associate the energies of nature and the incidents of life with figures of divine beauty. In technical skill, although not in charm of feeling, this poem is surpassed by "The Artists" ("Die Künstler"), which was planned and partly executed in Volkstädt. Schiller here sets forth in a series of brilliant sketches the part which the arts have played in the development of man. In expression, it marks the last stage in the transition from the tumultuous style of his youth to the noble and measured verse of his mature years.

CHAPTER VIII.

IN JENA.

A BRILLIANT reception awaited Schiller in Jena, for, as author of "The Robbers" and "Don Carlos," he had precisely the kind of reputation which was likely to appeal to the imagination of young students. He chose for the subject of his introductory lecture, "What is universal history, and for what end is it studied?" As the hour for the delivery of the lecture approached, the room became so overcrowded that it was necessary to move to a hall four times as large; and even this could not contain the multitude of eager youths who pressed to hear him. In the evening they met before his door, and played and sang in his honour, afterwards dispersing with hearty cheers.

Schiller lectured during his first term on ancient history, from primitive times to the age of Alexander the Great. Much of the ground being as new to himself as to his hearers, his lectures cost him a vast amount of labour; but he was, on the whole, satisfied with his new circumstances. He wrote to Körner that for the first time he felt "at home," that he had been kindly treated by his friends, and that his "humour" was "good." Early in August, Körner had occasion to be in Leipsic with his wife and sister-in-law; and although the work of the university was still going on, Schiller resolved to visit them and to bring them back with him to Jena. He went by Lauchstädt, where Caroline and Lotte had been for some time; the elder sister, who was in delicate health, having been advised to try the baths there. Caroline happened to be alone, and Schiller seized the opportunity to tell her of his love for Lotte, and to ask her whether he might hope that it would be returned. She was able to assure him that he had already won Lotte's heart, and that she would be proud and happy to be his wife. Overjoyed, Schiller pursued his journey; and on the evening of the same day he wrote from Leipsic: "Is it true, dearest Lotte? May I hope that Caroline has read your mind, and has responded from your heart to the feelings which I had not confidence to confess to you? Oh, how heavily has the secret weighed on me! —a secret which I have had to keep ever since we knew each other. Often, when we lived together, I summoned all my courage, and came to you with the intention of revealing it, but always my courage deserted me. I fancied there was selfishness in my wish; I feared that I was thinking only of my own happiness, and this thought drove me back. Confirm what Caroline has led me to hope. Tell me that you will be mine, and that my happiness does not cost you any sacrifice." "Caroline," answered Lotte, "*has* read my mind, and has responded from my heart. The thought that I may be able to contribute to your happiness stands before me clear and radiant."

A few days afterwards the sisters went to Leipsic with

a friend; and Schiller hoped that for his sake, as well as for her own, Lotte would become dear to Körner. But to his surprise and vexation, she was received rather coldly. Schiller had maintained absolute silence about his love, and this was resented by Körner, who regarded it as a sign of a strange want of confidence. The mis-understanding lasted for some months, and it seemed not impossible, from the increasing restraint in the tone of their letters, that they would gradually drift away from each other; but this misfortune was happily pre-vented. A few frank words on either side ultimately brought them together, and there was never again the slightest interruption to the free flow of their affection.

Schiller resumed his life in Jena with fresh hope: his work, his companionships, his plans, all were now seen in new lights. "I have just returned from a walk," he wrote in one of his letters. "In the great free space of nature, as in my solitary room, it is always the same ether in which I move, and the most beautiful landscape is only a mirror of the ever-abiding figure. Never have I felt so strongly how freely our minds play with nature, how little it gives us of itself, and how much it receives from our feeling. How often have I seen the sun set, and how often has my fancy lent it speech and soul! But never, never as now, have I read my love in it." On one occasion he interrupted himself in the preparation of a lecture to write to the sisters that he was made happy by the illusion that they were beside him. "When a Mohammedan prays," he added, "he turns his face towards Mecca. I think I must set up a desk in which I may turn mine towards Rudolstadt, for my religion and my prophet are there!"

The vacation Schiller spent in Volkstädt, where he occupied his old rooms; and every day he had the pleasure of seeing Lotte and her sister. As a rule, however, he could visit them only in the afternoon, for Frau von Lengefeld now lived in the palace, having been made governess of the children of the hereditary Prince of Rudolstadt, and her daughters generally spent the evening with her. Schiller was buoyed up by the anticipation that, during the approaching term, he would be able greatly to increase his income by private lectures; but he was soon undeceived. Only a small class was formed, and half of the students did not pay their fees, so that 60 thalers represented the whole of his gain for what would be a hard winter's work. Marriage, therefore, seemed to be far off, unless he could devise some new means of overcoming his difficulties. After thinking of various expedients, he at last resolved to apply to the Duke of Weimar for a fixed salary. The Duke asked Schiller to come to him, expressed his regret that he could not make a generous response, but offered to let him have 200 thalers a-year. This was miserable enough pay, even at that time, for such work as Schiller's; but with the money he might make by writing, and with Lotte's small fortune, he hoped that it might be adequate. As Lotte took his own sanguine view, there seemed to be no further reason for delay; and on the 18th of February 1790 he went to fetch his bride from Erfurt, where she and Caroline were visiting a friend. On the 22d the marriage was quietly celebrated in a small church in Wenigenjena, a village near Jena.

"What a beautiful life I lead now!" wrote Schiller

to Körner a week afterwards. " I look around me joyfully, and my heart finds outside of itself an enduring
source of soft contentment." About the same time
Lotte wrote to her cousin, Wilhelm von Wolzogen : " I
never imagined there was so much happiness in the
world as I now feel. In loving Schiller I am bound to
him by a thousand ties ; no one else could have given
me what I have in him ; and he, too, is happy, as my
heart tells me. Dear Wilhelm, who could have thought
that all this would happen when you brought my Schiller
to me for the first time ? Thanks to you ! Thanks, also,
to destiny, which gave me my happiness through you ! "
Nothing occurred to disturb their peace during this
year ; and Schiller began with confidence a new work,
his " History of the Thirty Years' War." It was intended for ' The Calendar,' a periodical issued by Göschen,
who offered him unusually high terms. All day, when
not engaged at the university, he laboured at this book ;
and before midsummer he had fought his way through
the preliminary difficulties, and brought the narrative
down to the career of Gustavus Adolphus. This part
was immediately published, and even the critical Körner,
who had not hitherto ranked Schiller very highly as a
historian, praised it enthusiastically.

Schiller was now near a long series of fiery trials, in
which the temper of his spirit was to be more severely
tested than in the worst hardships to which he had been
hitherto exposed. At the close of 1790 he and his wife
went for a short holiday to Erfurt ; and one evening,
after returning from a concert, he was attacked by a
feverish cold. For several days he was confined to his
room ; but, believing that he had quite recovered, he

soon returned to Jena, leaving Lotte to spend some time
in Weimar. Two days after his arrival he was again
ill, this time much more dangerously; and Lotte had to
hasten home. He spat blood, and in frequently recur-
ring spasms had so much difficulty in breathing, that
the bursting of a blood-vessel in the lungs seemed to
be almost inevitable. Day and night he had to be
carefully nursed; and he became so weak that the
slightest movement made him faint. By-and-by he
recovered slightly, and in spring he hoped that he was
rapidly advancing towards perfect health; but in May
1791 he was struck down by a still more terrible attack,
and his life was repeatedly despaired of. He lost his
voice, and could make his wishes known only by writing
with a feeble and trembling hand.

His health had never been very good, and it had been
prematurely injured by the harsh conditions of his early
manhood. From this time forward he was always more or
less an invalid, forced to be constantly on his guard, and
often apparently approaching his last hour. It was now
that the splendid elements of Schiller's character fully
disclosed themselves. However much he suffered, a harsh
or impatient word never crossed his lips, and a noble
resignation became his permanent mood. His fire and
enthusiasm were unquenched; but he became in manner
more tender, gentle, and sympathetic. To his passion
for heroic greatness he added a fine appreciation for those
sweet and gracious qualities which give an enduring
charm to the ordinary intercourse of life. His faults had
never been of a mean or petty character; but henceforth
he would have been incapable even of the slight touch
of jealousy with which he had contemplated for a time

the genius and good fortune of Goethe. Small and un-
worthy feelings seemed to have no mode of access to
that generous mind; he moved in a sphere too high and
pure for ignoble rivalries or base suspicions; and even
narrow natures expanded in the light and warmth of his
presence.

In July 1791 he was able to go with his wife and sister-
in-law to Carlsbad. As he was already meditating "Wallenstein," he gladly took the opportunity of visiting
Eger, where he saw the Rathhaus, with Wallenstein's
portrait, and the room in which he was murdered. He
was also pleased to obtain some idea of military manners
by making the acquaintance of several Austrian officers.
A portrait of him, sketched while he was at Carlsbad,
gives a vivid impression of his appearance at this time.
He is seated upon an ass, his right hand touching the
bridle, while with the left he holds the long pipe which
he is quietly smoking. He wears an immense hat,
broader than the broadest of "wideawakes;" and his
boots, the straps of which, at the top, are unfastened,
reach nearly to his knees. His form is meagre; and his
bent shoulders, over which his long hair flows, betoken
lamentable weakness. There is something childlike in
the expression of his delicate features, yet there is a suggestion of much past suffering in their look of patience,
kindness, and calm.

Late in autumn they were again in Jena, and he felt
well enough to translate the second and the fourth books
of the "Æneid." During this period of illness his recovery was retarded by renewed anxiety as to his circumstances,—for, as his resources diminished, his expenses
increased. Before the close of 1791, however, he was

delivered, by a sudden stroke, from all his perplexities, and enabled to face the future with a quiet and contented mind. In the previous year, the Danish writer, Jens Baggesen, had made his acquaintance, and had been attracted to him by an almost magical power. Never did a poet win more ardent love than that which Baggesen lavished on Schiller. Having returned to his own country, he talked incessantly of his hero to the hereditary Prince of Augustenburg and the Minister, Count von Schimmelmann; and they soon shared his enthusiasm. By-and-by Baggesen received an accurate account of Schiller's ill health and of his poverty, and he immediately submitted it to his powerful friends. To their eternal honour, they decided to give the poet an effective proof of their sympathy; and on the 13th of December 1791, he received from them a letter, conceived in a tone worthy of his own ideal spirit, informing him that 3000 thalers were at his service, to be paid to him by annual instalments of 1000 thalers. If a god had appeared before Schiller, he could hardly have been more surprised. For the first time he was now a free man. The load of debt which had so long crushed him to the earth might be rolled away; he could give himself time to recover his physical energies; and, as he wrote to Körner, it would be in his power "to work for immortality." The gift was offered in a way which, to a man of Schiller's temper, made the sense of obligation a pleasure; and he poured forth his gratitude in terms which must have caused his benefactors to feel that an act of kindness had never been more magnificently rewarded.

The year 1792 opened with bright hopes, and during

its course he was to be cheered by several pleasant incidents. In April he and his wife visited the Körners
in Dresden, and he had the satisfaction of seeing that
they at last did justice to Lotte's loyal, affectionate, and
poetic spirit. Later on he was delighted by a visit from
his mother and his youngest sister Nanette. Of his
mother, he wrote to Körner that she had, indeed,
changed during the previous ten years, but that, notwithstanding the illnesses through which she had passed,
she had the appearance of good health. "It rejoices
me," he added, "that this is so, and that I have her
near me and can make her happy." Nanette, who was
about fifteen years of age, he described as "still a child
of nature." She was a beautiful girl, gentle and un-
assuming, very thoughtful, and regarding her brother
with boundless admiration. She had not only studied
his works, but ardently desired to represent on the stage
those of his creations which touched her heart; and she
read his poems with so much feeling and expression, that
he was inclined to encourage her ambition. But the
destiny of this lovely nature, with its flower-like grace
and purity, was to fade and pass away in early youth.

In September Schiller was able to inform Körner that
he had despatched the last sheets of his "History of the
Thirty Years' War." "Now," he wrote, "I am free, and
will remain free for ever. No more work that another
imposes upon me, or that has not its origin in sympathy
and inclination!" His labours as a historian were thus
virtually finished, and he closed them mainly because
his mind was occupied by studies in which he was far
more deeply interested.

Germany had now fairly entered upon the great period

of her literature; and one of the deepest currents in the intellectual movement of the age was that which related to the ultimate problems of philosophy. An entirely new direction had been given to speculative thought by Kant, whose 'Critique of Pure Reason,' by the way, happened to be published in the same year as "The Robbers"—the year, too, of Lessing's death. Kant's bold and inspiring doctrines stirred quite as deep an interest as is stirred in our own time by the theory of evolution. Even Goethe, who hated metaphysics, was occasionally swept into the stream; and men who had an impulse towards philosophy, fancied that an intellectual evangel had been proclaimed, which would soon revolutionise the world.

Schiller was of too open and alert an intelligence not to be quickly influenced by ideas which were everywhere in the air. As we have seen, he had been brought into some contact with Kant's principles by Körner, who was one of the philosopher's earliest and most enthusiastic adherents. In Jena he could not, if he would, have been altogether indifferent to the new teaching; for Jena was one of the great centres of contemporary thought; and Reinhold, a leading professor of the university, and Schiller's friend, devoted his life to the exposition of the critical philosophy. For some time, however, Schiller was too much absorbed by his special pursuits to attack so formidable a subject with all his strength: not till he began to recover from his first illness in the spring of 1791 did he find leisure to turn to it with a determination to master it. He then studied 'The Critique of Judgment,' and for several years afterwards his mind was penetrated by the critical philosophy in one or other of its aspects.

It was not by accident that Schiller began with 'The Critique of Judgment.' He was one of those poets who cannot help reflecting on the impression produced by their work, and on the laws of the poetic faculty. For many years—ever since he had been a pupil in Professor Abel's class—the subject had attracted him from time to time; and he had extended his inquiries over the whole field of æsthetic philosophy. Naturally, therefore, he applied himself first to the work in which Kant was on ground more or less familiar to him; and to the end the critical philosophy interested him most of all in its relation to the principles of æsthetics. He intended to embody his ideas on art in a dialogue with the title "Callias; or, Concerning Beauty" ("Kallias; oder, über die Schönheit"); and we may well regret that he did not execute a scheme which would have given scope both for fancy and for reason. Instead of "Callias" he wrote his letters "Concerning the Æsthetic Education of Man" ("Ueber die ästhetische Erziehung des Menschen"). These letters he addressed, as a mark of gratitude, to the Prince of Augustenburg.

Until 1790 he had continued to issue 'Thalia' at irregular intervals, finding it a useful medium for the publication of various writings, mainly historical, which he did not deem worthy of an independent existence. Twelve numbers had appeared. In 1792 he projected another periodical of a similar kind, 'The New Thalia' ('Die Neue Thalia'), of which two volumes were to be issued annually, each volume including six numbers. In about two years this miscellany also died; but it contained much good work, of which the best related to what were now Schiller's favourite studies.

In November 1792 Schiller ventured to return to his professorial work; but now he chose as the subject of his private prelections, not history, but æsthetic philosophy. As his class was well attended, and most of the students paid their fees—a louis-d'or each—he would have been well satisfied if his health had been tolerable. But it was sadly broken, and in the spring of 1793 he was overtaken by one of his spasms in the midst of a lecture. The course was stopped, and he withdrew with his wife to a country-house near Jena. His recovery, however, being slow, he resolved to try whether he might not profit by his native air—a decision to which in any case he was inclined in consequence of his parting promise to his mother.

Schiller's was not one of those natures which delight in recalling the scenes and experiences of youth. His sanguine and aspiring temperament led him rather to dwell on the future, and to regard the past and the present as but necessary stages in his progress towards a more glorious goal. Hence he does not seem to have been much excited by the prospect of revisiting his early home, or to have occupied himself in contrasting "then" and "now." Early in August 1792 he and his wife started on their journey in a carriage bought for the occasion, making in the first instance for Heilbronn. Here they were joined by Caroline, who happened to be staying in Würtemberg, and by Schiller's sister, Louise, who for the time kept house for them. Their original purpose was to make Heilbronn their head-quarters; but in about a month they moved to Ludwigs-burg, and afterwards they took up their abode in Stutt-gart, which they liked better than either of the two other towns. At Ludwigsburg a great event happened—the birth of their first child, a son. Schiller was precisely the man to feel all the charm and joy of this new experience. His first-born opened in his heart a deep fountain of tenderness, and in his grand manner he instantly began to form large schemes for the child's education. The budding possibilities of this new life would be evolved, he determined, in accordance with the principles of Quintilian, whom he happened to be at that time studying.

The elder Schiller was now in his seventieth year, but his life had been so temperate and active that he hardly seemed to be sixty. Keenly vexed and irritated the old man had been by his son's wayward course; but now that Friedrich had returned to him a professor, a famous man, and the friend of famous men, he forgot past errors, and was even ready to confess that the youth who had seemed so foolish had perhaps best understood the career for which he was adapted. Schiller was a Hofrath, too, having received this title before his marriage from the Duke of Meiningen; and the distinction was one which flattered some of his father's most cherished prejudices. Altogether, there had probably never been between father and son such free and affectionate communion of spirit as they now enjoyed. Schiller's mother had always understood him rightly, and her happiness in his society was without check in presence of the softened humour of her rugged old husband.

While Schiller was in Würtemberg, his old patron and oppressor, the Duke, died. Schiller had written to him, but had received no answer. According to Von Hoven, Schiller visited his grave, and spoke tenderly of one who

had been so prominent a figure in his history; but there
is no trace of kindness in the letter in which he spoke of
the event to Körner. "The death of the old Herod,"
he wrote, "has no influence either upon me or upon my
family, except that it is well for all who, like my father,
stand in direct relation with the sovereign, to have to
deal with a *man*. That the new Duke is in every good,
and in every bad, sense of the word."

Schiller continued to meditate deeply on the questions
which had engaged his thoughts before he left home, and
wrote several of the letters on "Æsthetic Education."
He had, however, many dark and troubled hours, for
his native air proved to have less reviving power than
he had expected. Frequent attacks of his old malady
laid him low, some of them being so severe that the
onlookers often expected to see him suffocated in one of
his paroxysms. "Heaven grant," he wrote to Körner,
"that my patience may not give way, and that a life
which is so often interrupted by a true death may still
have some value for me!" But in the end he benefited
considerably by his visit; and when, in the middle of
May 1794, he found himself once more in Jena, he was
able to hope that he might still achieve the aims to
which his energies were henceforth to be dedicated.

Since Schiller went to Weimar in search of better
fortunes, the civilised world had been shaken to its centre
by the French Revolution. At first he did not follow
its events closely, for, as he wrote to Wilhelm von Wolzogen, who was in Paris, he felt that his capacity for the
judgment of public affairs "had not been exercised, had
not been developed." As the convulsion became more
terrible, however, he watched its progress with growing

interest; and to a slight extent he himself was brought
into personal relation with it, the National Assembly
having selected him as one of those foreign writers who
were considered worthy of the honour of French citizenship.[1] For some time the party of change had his full
sympathy, but he was alarmed and horrified by the ex-
cesses of the Convention. He even began to write a
defence of Louis XVI., and was not without hope that
the voice of a disinterested spectator would have some
effect on French opinion. Before he had finished his
defence the king was executed. "For fourteen days,"
he wrote to Körner, after he had been startled, like all
the world, by this event, "I have been unable to look at
a newspaper—these butchers disgust me so!"

The Reign of Terror confirmed Schiller in his bitter repugnance; and in his later writings he uttered
frequent warnings against revolutionary methods. He
had no sympathy, however, with those whom fear of
revolution drove into reaction. He had long held,
and continued to the end to hold, that laws should
originate in the will of the people by whom they are
to be obeyed; and to this he added the vital doctrine
(about which he was even more in earnest) that,
whatever may be the source of authority, the natural
impulses of mankind should be subjected only to such

[1] Schiller was known in France by a translation, or "adapta-
tion," of "The Robbers;" but the notions about him beyond the
Rhine must have been vague, for the proceedings relating to the
honour conferred on him were thus reported in the 'Moniteur:' "Un
membre demande que le Sieur *Gille*, publiciste allemand, soit compris
dans la liste de ceux à qui l'Assemblée vient d'accorder le titre de
citoyen Français: cette demande est adoptée." The diploma, coun-
tersigned by Danton, and accompanied by a letter from Roland, did
not reach Schiller for five years.

restraint as is demanded by the general welfare. Half of
the difficulties in the world sprang, he thought, from the
incessant intermeddling of Governments with the relations
between man and man. To him, as to most of the great
thinkers of the eighteenth century, the individual was
far more sacred than the State; and the State, in his
opinion, performed its part most wisely by confining its
functions within the strictest possible limits. Modern
Socialists contend that this view might be defensible if
all men started in life with equal capacities and equal
opportunities, but that in the existing condition of the
world the State is the only power by which the weak
can be delivered from the oppression of the strong. To
this Schiller would have replied that the true remedy
for the inequalities of fortune is to be found, not in
external control, but in the growth of a spirit of humanity and self-sacrifice. And he had always an ardent
faith that, if men were but let alone, such a spirit would
more and more dominate their conduct. There was not
the faintest approach to the pessimistic creed in his
estimate of the influences which, in the last resort, move
mankind ; he judged others in the light of his own sympathies, and was, moreover, sustained by the belief that
unseen powers determine the progress of the world, and
are gradually directing it towards worthy ends.

Before the French Revolution there was hardly any
sentiment which Schiller held in such light esteem as
patriotism. "We moderns," he wrote to Körner in
1788, "have within our reach a kind of interest which
was unknown to the Greeks and the Romans, and with
which the interest of patriotism cannot be for a moment
compared. The latter is important only for immature

nations, for the youth of the world." In the hour of Germany's humiliation he modified this hasty judgment. Then he began to take pride in the German name, and to prophesy that the time would come when "the slowest people in Europe would overtake the most swift." "The German," he wrote, "has been unfortunate in war; but that in which his worth consists he has not lost. The German empire and the German nation are two very different things."

112

CHAPTER IX.

THE greater number of Schiller's prose works were produced in the interval between his departure from Mannheim in 1785 and his return from Würtemberg to Jena
in 1794. A few were written afterwards, but even they
express ideas which were the result of thought and re-
search during this period. As a prose writer he takes
high rank in German literature, for he left hardly any
of his subjects in the exact position in which he found
them. His style has not the grace and simplicity of
which Goethe was so perfect a master; nor has it the
vivid, almost dramatic force of Lessing's manner. It
is the style of an orator, free, flowing, too rhetorical
sometimes, but quite as often stately, and even majestic.
He seldom aims at delicate effects ; he prefers to group
his facts and ideas in masses, and to produce broad,
general impressions. The full energy of his best passages can be realised only when they are read aloud ;
and this is perhaps as true of his verse as of his prose.

His prose writings include, among other essays in
criticism, a review of Goethe's "Egmont," a paper on

Bürger's poems, and a series of letters on his own "Don Carlos." These essays, although presenting a very in-adequate estimate of the works with which they deal, throw much light on Schiller's conception of the aims and laws of poetry. A work of a different class, "The Philosophical Letters," possesses a stronger interest, be-cause of the hints it affords regarding the religious opinions with which Schiller satisfied himself in early manhood. The correspondence is supposed to pass be-tween two friends, Julius and Raphael, who love each other with a fervour which was more characteristic of friendship in ancient times than in the conventional modern world. One of the letters contains a confession of faith, in which the writer expresses a doctrine that verges closely on pantheism.

The only prose tale of any importance written by Schiller is "The Visionary," which he never completed. The hero is a prince, the heir to a German throne; and when the story opens, he has been for some time living in retirement in Venice. He belongs to the Lutheran Church, but, although given to quiet meditation, he has never subjected his faith to rigid scrutiny; and he has a decided leaning towards superstition. To this prince, for the sake of the position he will inherit, certain Catholic leaders direct their attention; and the object of the tale is to unfold the means by which he is at last driven to seek for refuge from intolerable difficulties in the bosom of the Roman Church. The plot is extrava-gant and fantastic; but in style the story is admirable, flowing on without interruption in a broad, limpid stream; and there are passages of almost fascinating interest. Such are some of the scenes in which the

prince appears to be caught in the meshes of preter-
natural intrigue, and all of those which relate to his
love for the woman who first touches his ideal. When
"The Visionary" appeared in 'Thalia,' it contained a
long philosophical conversation (afterwards much shortened), which is also of some value, for it sets forth
many of the conclusions at which Schiller arrived
after the period represented by "The Philosophical
Letters." The leading idea is, that man, alone of
beings known to us, has the power of merging his
individual impulses in the life of his species; that in
proportion as he exercises this power he is noble and
happy, while in proportion as he neglects the life of his
species, and thinks only of his personal pleasures, he
allies himself to the lower animals and becomes common
and wretched. For conceptions of this nature Schiller
appears to have been partly indebted to Moritz, a suggestive writer with whom he was personally acquainted;
and, to a certain extent, they connect themselves more
easily than some of his later speculations with the dis-
tinctive thought of the nineteenth century.

Had Schiller not been a great poet, it is improbable
that his historical writings would have survived : it is,
however, generally acknowledged that they have sterling
merits. In the eighteenth century Germany could boast
of few historians,—a fact which Lessing explained by
pointing out that German men of letters would not
study, while scholars could not write well. A deeper
reason, perhaps, was, that the absence of political life in
Germany prevented even intelligent men from taking
much interest in the progress of events, either in their

own or in past times.   Schiller was among the earliest
German writers who attempted to make ordinary readers
feel the charm of history, and his endeavours were attended by considerable success.   His historical works
do not embody the results of profound investigation;
but he honestly consulted the most important authorities, and always knew how to make his narrative intelligible.   His studies exercised a decisive influence
on his later and more important labours, for they not
only led him to choose historical subjects for dramatic
treatment, but provided him with materials on which
his imagination could work freely.

His account of the revolt of the Netherlands ('Geschichte des Abfalls der vereinigten Niederlande von der
Spanischen Regierung') was the first, and it is in some
respects the best, of his histories.   He had only recently
finished "Don Carlos," and his mind was still filled with
the ideas and sentiments for which he had created so
brilliant a representative in the Marquis Posa.   He undertook, therefore, with enthusiasm to trace the progress
of a great conflict for liberty; and his enthusiasm gave
warmth and animation to his style.   The larger portion
of the book he wrote in Volkstädt, generally reading in
the evening to his friends in Rudolstadt the passages
which he had completed in the course of the day; and
this, no doubt, helped to sustain the interest with which
he entered upon his task.   Unfortunately he did not
carry the history beyond the arrival of Alva in the
Netherlands, when the prospects of freedom appeared
to be darkest; but the period within which he confines
himself is capable of being represented as a whole, and
he moves over the ground with the firm step of one who

knows it intimately. Here Philip II. appears in his
true colours as a dark, narrow, and ruthless egoist, in
whose nature religion itself becomes stern and cruel.
William of Orange may almost be called the hero of the
work; and perhaps no other historian, within the same
limits, has presented so vivid a picture of his reserved
and powerful character, and of the sources of his influence over less original minds. Scarcely less effective
is Schiller's description of the gay, courageous, and fascinating Egmont. While he gives due prominence to
these and other actors in the mighty drama, he does
not lose sight of the historical tendencies which were
behind individual conduct; and he secures breadth for
his narrative by connecting it with the general stream
of progress.

Schiller was attracted to the Thirty Years' War by
essentially the same elements as those which interested
him in the revolt of the Netherlands. With the
creed of the Protestants of the seventeenth century he
had as little sympathy as with that of their opponents;
but they were fighting for spiritual freedom, and this
was the cause which of all others appealed to Schiller
most powerfully. In his history, however ('Geschichte
des Dreissigjährigen Krieges'), he was able to follow
the course of events more calmly than in his previous
work; so that, if the colours of his picture are less
bright, its outlines are traced with a surer hand. As
the periodical in which the history appeared was to be
stopped, Schiller was compelled to hurry over the later
portion of his subject; but this is not much to be
regretted, as he found little to interest him in periods
which were not dominated by great minds. Since his

time new light has been thrown on every stage of the
Thirty Years' War, especially on the Catholic reaction
which produced, and was in turn modified by, Ferdinand II. It is still, however, possible to read with
pleasure Schiller's broad sketches of the state of Europe
at the time of the war; and his description of the
heroic career of Gustavus Adolphus is too full of life
and sympathy ever to lose its interest. There is also
remarkable insight in his study of the moody and wayward Wallenstein. Schiller pauses less frequently than
in his work on the Netherlands to analyse character, but
he is at more pains to bring out in action the qualities
of the leading figures.

While in Weimar, Schiller began to issue a series of
"Memoirs," and to these he contributed introductory
essays, some of which he regarded as his masterpieces in
this kind. None of them, however, have more original
force than the lecture with which he opened his career
as a professor. Here he emphasises the fact that, besides
the history of individual countries and movements, there
is a wider and more philosophical study—"universal
history." This lecture excited the enthusiasm of his
students by the largeness of its doctrines and the animating hopefulness of its tone ; and it is one of the land-
marks which indicate the utmost verge of speculation
on its subject, before the philosophy of history received
a new impetus from the science of language, political
economy, and the general principles of evolution.

Schiller found sincere pleasure in historical studies,
but he was not sorry to give them up in favour of philosophical speculation ; for there were multitudes of ques-

tions about which he had reflected since early youth
without arriving at any final decision, and respecting
which it seemed possible to obtain new light through
the critical philosophy.   In all his reasonings he started
from Kant, but his intellect was too vigorous and independent to satisfy itself with mere acquiescence in the
conclusions of a master.   Every great subject with which
philosophy concerns itself he thought out for himself,
deriving aid from other writers as well as from Kant—
mainly, perhaps, from Lessing, Herder, and Fichte.

The tendency of the philosophy of the age was to
present an exalted conception of human greatness.   To
Kant, Space and Time were but forms of sense, while the
universe, according to his system, could not enter consciousness except by adapting itself to the categories of
the understanding.   Fichte, advancing further, found
that the phenomenal world was the free creation of the
individual mind working in accordance with its own
laws.   Schiller shared to the utmost this tendency, which
harmonised with all his modes of thought and with all
the peculiarities of his character.   He, too, gave the
facts of existence a purely ideal interpretation; and in
that individuality, in whose depths were such vast energies, he saw a power too great and too sacred to be subjected to arbitrary external control.   No one, however,
could have a stronger faith in the moral order which is
above the individual will; and he recognised as an essential element of human consciousness those fears, hopes,
and aspirations which are appealed to by the various
forms of religious belief and feeling.

These characteristics find more or less distinct expression in his poetry; but in his philosophical writings

he limits himself to the discussion of the æsthetic emotions, their origin, their laws, and their effect on human life, with an occasional reference to matters bearing on ethics. A complete system of æsthetics he did not expound, nor perhaps did he ever find a perfectly satisfactory solution of the problems which interested him; but his essays contain many suggestive hints, and they have exercised considerable influence on later German thought.

Among the most attractive of his papers on subjects of this class is an essay on "Grace and Dignity" ("Ueber die Anmuth und Würde"), published in 'New Thalia' in 1793. Kant had represented Duty as a stern mistress, confronting man with a threatening aspect, and demanding that he shall submit to her decrees with a conscious acknowledgment of her authority. In this paper Schiller admits the validity of Kant's conception in certain stages of human development, but insists that there is a still higher conception—that, namely, of a nature which conforms to the law of reason without effort; a nature in which duty has become instinct, and which has a consciousness of joy and freedom only in worthy action. In such a nature—"the beautiful soul"—there is no discord; every element of humanity, the sensuous and the spiritual, receiving the satisfaction which accords with the scheme of the whole. Grace, or beautiful movement, Schiller regards as the manifestation of this harmonious working of human powers. But man's will is liable to be attacked by stormy passions, the force of which he cannot but feel. Dignity is defined by Schiller as the expression of the power by which man rises and asserts his freedom against these passions, driving them back within the limits prescribed by reason. If grace and

dignity at their highest stage could be united in one
person—the former supported by beauty of structure, the
latter by force—we should have the ideal of the human
form. "According to this ideal of beauty the ancient
marbles were formed, and we may recognise it in the
divine form of a Niobe, in the Apollo Belvedere, in the
winged genius of the Borghese, and in the Muse of the
Barberini Palace." Schiller concludes his essay by some
fine and interesting suggestions as to the part which
may be properly played in the intercourse of life by
grace and dignity,—now one, now the other, being pre-
dominant, or both acting together in unison.

A more elaborate work is the series of letters "Concerning the Æsthetic Education of Man" ("Ueber die
ästhetische Erziehung des Menschen"). These letters,
published in 1794-95, were partly written after Schiller's
return from Würtemberg. There are twenty-seven of
them, and they appeared in three instalments, the first
consisting of nine letters, the second of seven, the third
of eleven. In style the work is as near perfection as
anything Schiller ever wrote, the first nine letters being
especially remarkable for that union of grace and dignity
which he so much admired in human expression. He
starts with a reference to what he conceives to be the
central effort of modern times : it is, he thinks, the
effort to transform the State from the mere condition of
nature to a condition in which it will accord with reason.
He expresses complete sympathy with this aim, but
points to the vast obstacles which stand in the way,—
obstacles arising partly from the fact that the mass of
the humbler classes are materialised, while the higher
classes manifest a refined egoism, governing conduct

only by conventional rules. Besides, the modern man has almost lost the idea of that free and harmonious play of all his powers which characterised Greek life. Each has his special work, and only in rare cases does any one think of going beyond the limits of his customary activity. By this minute division and subdivision of labour, humanity may have been enriched, but the individual has been impoverished. By what force, then, can it be hoped that a reasonable form of society will be evolved? It is useless to appeal to the State, since the State is partly responsible for existing evils; and it can itself become worthy only through an enlightened community. Schiller concludes the first section of his argument by stating his belief that the power which will be most effective in leading man to the life to which he aspires is Art. In the second part he tries to prove his position by indicating the essential nature of beauty. In man he finds two fundamental elements, the sensuous and the spiritual. But there is a third impulse—the impulse towards play; and Schiller boldly maintains that man is man in the fullest sense only when he plays. The Greeks, he says, understood this, and hence they banished from the face of their gods every trace of care and labour. In this impulse towards play art has its root, and in order to satisfy its demands the artist must combine both sense and spirit, giving to each the place which is its due in the order of its importance. Art, therefore, touches the whole being of man; and it is because it does so that we may look to it to help the world to higher forms of social and individual life. In the last part Schiller gives fuller expression to the idea that the tendency of true art is to

make us conscious, not only of this or that capacity, but
of all our energies. "If we have given ourselves," he
says, "to the enjoyment of genuine beauty, we are at
such a moment masters both of our passive and of
our active powers, and we shall be able to turn with
equal ease to work or play, to rest or movement, to submission or resistance, to observation or abstract thought."
In order that our mood may be made as general as possible, each art, while retaining its peculiarities, ought to
borrow as much as its conditions permit from the sister
arts. "Music in its highest perfection must become
form, and affect us with the calm power of the antique;
plastic art must become music, and move us by immediate sensuous impression; poetry must lay hold of us
powerfully like music, but at the same time encompass
us, like plastic art, with calm clearness." Moreover,
each art ought as far as possible to escape from the
limits imposed upon it by the material with which it
works. "In a truly beautiful work of art matter is
nothing, form everything, for through form alone the
whole nature of man is affected, through matter only
particular powers. Matter, however sublime and widely
comprehensive it may be, has a narrowing influence on
the mind, and from form alone true artistic freedom is
to be expected." Towards the conclusion of the work,
returning in part to the ideas of his essay on "Grace and
Dignity," he develops the doctrine that beauty ought not
to be confined to works of art, but should be made the
animating principle of the whole of human life. Thus
both the sensuous and the spiritual would receive their
rights, and "taste would bring harmony into society,
because it would create harmony in the individual." As

yet, however, society ruled by beauty is to be found,
"like the pure Church and the pure republic," only "in
a few select circles, where man guides his conduct, not by
mindless imitation of foreign manners, but in accordance
with his own beautiful nature ; where he walks through
the most confused relations with bold simplicity and
calm innocence, and needs neither to limit the freedom
of others in order to maintain his own, nor to cast aside
his dignity in order to manifest his grace."

One of the most important of Schiller's prose writings
is his treatise " On Naïve and Sentimental Poetry " [1]
("Ueber die Naive und Sentimentalische Dichtung"),
published in 1795-96,—like the " Æsthetic Letters," in
three instalments. This work is a remarkable example
of Schiller's power of placing in fresh lights every subject in which he interested himself : it is full of ideas
which were then new, and at the same time suggests
that the writer has only half revealed the wealth of his
thought.   He remarks on the passionate interest with
which modern minds view the spectacle of nature, and
points out that there is no trace of this feeling in Greek
literature. Whence this contrast?   Schiller finds the
explanation in the fact that, in modern times, life has
been so completely divorced from nature that the physical
world charms us by reminding us of our lost truth and
simplicity. In like manner we are moved by every manifestation of natural impulse, whether in children or in
persons of mature years who retain a childlike heart ;
and so we arrive at the conception of the "naïve," which

---

[1] The words "naïve " and "sentimental " are rather unfortunate,
but there seem to be no precise equivalents in English for the
terms used by Schiller.

Schiller defines as "nature standing in contrast with art
and putting it to shame." The naïve poet is one who
is himself so perfectly in harmony with nature that
he accepts the world as it is, and who in his poetry
reproduces the facts of life with absolute fidelity, not
mingling with his representation any element from his
own feeling. "The object completely possesses him;
his heart does not lie, like a bad metal, immediately
under the surface, but must, like gold, be sought for
in the depths. As the divinity behind the world,
so the naïve poet stands behind his work; he and
his work are one." As the greatest of naïve poets,
Homer and Shakespeare are mentioned; and it is here
that Schiller refers to the difficulty which he experi-
enced in youth in appreciating Shakespeare's greatness.
Misled by later writers, he had been accustomed to
seek first of all for the poet in his works, to feel the
throbbing of his heart, to reflect along with him on his
theme,—"in short, to view the object in the subject;"
and it was intolerable to him that in Shakespeare's
writings "the poet would never let himself be caught,
would never talk with his reader." "For several years,"
adds Schiller, "I studied Shakespeare, and gave him my
entire reverence, before his individuality became dear to
me." In opposition to the naïve poet, the "sentimental"
poet does not reflect the object as it is; he sees it in the
light of his own feelings, and mingles with his representation of it something of his individual character.
Nature is the eternal source of all poetry; but while
the naïve poet *is* nature, the sentimental poet only *seeks*
for her. Conscious of discord in the world, and in his
intellectual life, the sentimental poet strives to recover

unity, not by imitation of the actual, but by taking
refuge in the ideal, with which he brings the actual into
relation. As the ideal belongs to the infinite, he can
never present the perfection of form reached by the
naïve poet, who limits himself to the finite.   The
excellence of the latter consists in the absolute attain-
ment of a finite, that of the former in the approach to an
infinite, greatness.   Both kinds of poetry are legitimate,
and, properly interpreted, they exhaust every possible
species of imaginative effort.   Ancient poetry is not
without sentimental elements; and naïve poetry reappears from time to time in the modern world.   Still,
the distinction broadly marks the difference between
ancient and modern writers.   " The former appeal to us
by nature, by sensuous truth, by living impressions; the
latter appeal to us by ideas."   In essence the impression
produced by naïve poets is the same, in whatever department they work, whether in the lyric, in the epic,
in narrative poetry, or in the drama; but as the poetry
of sentiment deals with two elements, the ideal and the
actual, and their relations, many different kinds of effect
are open to it.   If the poet of sentiment makes reality
his main subject, although with the ideal in the background, he becomes satirical; and his satire may be
either pathetic or witty,—pathetic, if his mind is of the
order which touches the sublime; witty, if he tends
rather towards beauty than towards sublimity.   If, on
the other hand, the poet of sentiment directs his
thoughts mainly to the ideal, he becomes elegiac; and
he, too, may approach his theme in one of two ways.
Either nature and the ideal are a subject of sorrow,
because nature is lost, and the ideal is unattained; or

he may delight to represent them as united in the realm of imagination. From the former mood springs the elegy in the ordinary sense, from the latter the idyll in its widest significance. Starting from these definitions, Schiller offers a series of masterly criticisms of various modern writers, among others Goethe, in whom he recognises the rare power of giving naïve form to matter of a sentimental nature, thus combining the antique and the modern spirit. He also indicates the special danger of the sentimental and the naïve poet; the naïve poet (unless he happens to have a beautiful environment) being apt to fall into commonplace, the sentimental poet having a tendency to lose himself in extravagance.

This essay is the most original of Schiller's prose works, and it produced a stronger impression than any of the rest. In Goethe's opinion, it laid the foundation of modern criticism, since, although under different names, it first brought to view the vital distinction between the Hellenic and the Romantic methods. "The Schlegels," said Goethe to Eckermann, "seized the idea and pushed it further; so that all the world is now familiar with it, and everybody talks of Classicism and Romanticism, of which no one thought fifty years ago."

CHAPTER X.

SCHILLER AND GOETHE.

WE have now reached the last period of Schiller's life, the period of his highest and most brilliant creative activity. When he returned to Jena from Würtemberg he was in his thirty-fifth year, with health permanently broken, but with spiritual energy unabated, and with an inward calm which contrasted strongly with the restless vehemence of his early years. Henceforth there were few external changes in his career, and his history is in the main the history of his writings.

Jena was at this time as attractive a place of residence for Schiller as any in which he could have been settled, for it contained many distinguished men, with whom he was able to have friendly intercourse. Of these the chief was Wilhelm von Humboldt, who had married an intimate friend of Schiller's wife. He was a man of pleasant, jovial manners, and, although nearly eight years younger than Schiller, had already given evidence of the qualities which were afterwards to make him one of the deepest scholars and soundest statesmen of his age. Schiller loved no man more warmly; and Humboldt went to live for a time in Jena, chiefly for the purpose of being near his friend. Fichte had recently succeeded Reinhold as a professor of metaphysics, and Schiller saw him often, and was impressed by the bold-ness of his philosophical doctrines. By-and-by a new and still more advanced philosophy was being proclaimed in Jena by Schelling; and the Romantic school was soon to be founded there amid clamour and excitement by the brothers Schlegel. These and other writers, more or less sympathetic to him, Schiller had many opportunities of talking with; and he was invariably among those who took the lead in any society he entered. He delighted in conversation, and, whatever subject might be started, he seldom failed to generalise it, and to make it the occasion of an animated discussion. Ac-cording to the testimony of his friends, his talk was always bright and suggestive; and he was a sufficiently good listener to give a chance to everybody who had really anything to say.

With Körner he continued to maintain a constant correspondence; but he now formed a friendship which was to become of infinitely more importance to him than any he had hitherto known. This was his friendship with Goethe. He had repeatedly talked with Goethe since their first meeting in the house of Frau von Lenge-feld; but each had held aloof from the other, and there seemed to be no chance of their ever becoming intimate. One summer evening in 1794, returning from a meeting of a scientific society in Jena, of which they were hon-orary members, they happened to walk along together. Talking of the society, Schiller remarked that its mode of dealing with nature was too fragmentary to be of much use to the layman in science. Goethe answered that it was perhaps not better adapted to the initiated. A truer way, he added, was to regard nature as living and active, working from the whole into the parts ; but Schiller would not admit that this was a doctrine based on experience. Anxious to pursue the conversation, Goethe entered Schiller's house, and began to expound his theory of the metamorphosis of plants. Schiller listened attentively, but observed, "That is not experience, it is an idea." "Then," answered Goethe, rather provoked, " I am glad that I have ideas without knowing it, and even see them with my eyes." This conversation interested Goethe for the first time in Schiller, and made him wish that they should be better acquainted. Soon afterwards they met again, and Schiller wrote to Körner that they had talked much "about art, and the theory of art." " We found," he added, " an unexpected agreement in our ideas, which was the more interesting, because it proceeded from the greatest difference in our points of view."

In September 1794 they had approached each other so closely, that Goethe begged Schiller to spend a fortnight with him in Weimar ; and as Lotte was in Rudolstadt with her little boy, the invitation was gladly accepted. This visit made them absolutely sure of each other ; and ever afterwards, until Schiller's death, they maintained the closest intimacy,—exchanging ideas on all subjects of human interest—spurring one another to the utmost activity of their faculties. In all literary history there is nothing more beautiful than the friendship of these radiant spirits. Their sympathy was never darkened even by a passing shade of envy or jealousy ; each found pure delight in the greatness of the other ;

and, that each might be helped by the other's influence, to do justice to his genius was the continual hope and aim of both. To go to Jena and pass some evenings with his friend was one of Goethe's highest pleasures; and in Goethe's presence all that was best in Schiller's nature gleamed and sparkled. "It is astonishing," wrote Lotte, "what an influence Goethe's presence has on Schiller, and what an animating effect the frequent interchange of ideas with Goethe has upon him. He is quite different even if he is only in Weimar."

For a long time science had absorbed Goethe's energies, and he seemed to have lost sight of his true destiny. The consciousness of his poetical faculty, and a longing for its exercise, were rekindled by Schiller's enthusiasm; and in association with one whom he loved so well, and who so well deserved his love, he resumed the career in which he had still to achieve some of his highest triumphs. To Schiller he owed, to use his own words, "a new Spring." "You have created for me," he wrote, "a second youth, and have again made me a poet, which I had almost ceased to be." Most amply did Goethe repay the obligation, as Schiller again and again acknowledged. Schiller's tendency was to be too absorbed in his ideal world: in intercourse with Goethe he was compelled to descend from his cloudland, to present his abstract conceptions in concrete forms, to compare his ideas with facts, to observe, to classify. His whole method of thinking was thus modified; it became more direct, more animated, more fruitful. His poetry was also deeply influenced. Idealism which is not maintained in living contact with nature is apt to end in mannerism; and although Schiller's imagination was too powerful ever to content itself

with shadowy and unreal forms, it was in this direction
that his peril lay.   Goethe helped him to become conscious of it, and to strive against it.   An idealist he
could not but be : his idealism sprang from the inmost
conditions of his intellectual and moral nature.   But,
thanks in part to Goethe, the idealistic elements of his
genius were henceforth to be balanced by other elements,
more solid, more varied, and equally necessary for great
art.

Meanwhile Schiller had entered upon a new undertaking, which was to be the chief means of bringing the
two poets into close relation.   With the year 1794 the
help which had been so generously accorded him by the
Prince of Augustenburg and Count von Schimmelmann
would cease, so that it was necessary to find other ways
of enlarging his income.   He decided to issue a new
periodical, to be called the ' Horen ' ('Horæ').   His
friend Cotta not only expressed his willingness to publish it, but engaged to give him a salary of 1000 thalers
a-year, besides paying him for his contributions.   Schiller
formed a large scheme, and received promises of co-opera-
tion from most of the leading men of letters in Germany.
Among others he applied for contributions to Goethe,
who replied, with unusual warmth, that he would look
forward with pleasure to his connection with the new
magazine.   For the ' Horen ' Schiller wrote all the philosophical articles that had not appeared in ' New Thalia ; '
and he contributed to it, besides poems, an excellent
historical article depicting the siege of Antwerp — an
article which he afterwards appended to his history of
the revolt of the Netherlands.   The enterprise cost him
far more labour than he anticipated, as few of those who

had pledged themselves to aid him kept their promise;
and in less than four years he was glad to let the
' Horen ' die.

In 1795 Schiller conceived another scheme—that of
issuing a yearly volume of lyrics, to be called the ' Almanac of the Muses ' ('Musenalmanach'). Here again
Goethe, with whom he was now intimate, undertook
to help him; and Schiller worked at the details of his
undertaking with even more than his usual enthusiasm.
A good many years had passed since he had abandoned
poetry, first for history, afterwards for philosophy. Philosophy now began to be distasteful to him; he found it
barren and dreary, and longed for the brighter world of
free and living forms. ' Wilhelm Meister,' the first part
of which had been recently published, confirmed and
deepened this feeling. "I cannot express to you," he
wrote to Goethe, "how painful it often is to me to glance
from a product of this kind into the philosophical sphere.
There all is so cheerful, so living, so harmoniously solved,
so humanly true; here all is so severe, so rigid and abstract, so utterly unnatural; for while all nature is syn-
thesis, all philosophy is antithesis. The poet is the
only true *man*, and the best philosopher, compared with
him, is but a caricature." The 'Almanac,' therefore,
offered itself to Schiller at the right moment; and while
writing his essay on 'Naïve and Sentimental Poetry,' he
interrupted his labour from time to time to give free
course to his ideas in verse. His genius was so extraor-
dinarily productive after its long repose, that before the
end of the year 1795 he had written upwards of forty
poems, some of them of considerable length.

Nearly all of these pieces have a more or less definite

relation to the stage of intellectual life through which
Schiller had just passed : they are the poetical rendering
of the ideas which he had set forth in prose. They
necessarily appeal to a select class, for they contain few
elements which touch ordinary experience ; and only
some of them please the imagination with living pictures. They are not, however, didactic poems ; for
Schiller's object is rather to express the feeling which
his ideas excite, than to present the ideas themselves.
His feeling is always high and noble, and its force is
seldom broken by any imperfection either in his diction
or in his rhythm. Perhaps the most characteristic of
the series is the well-known poem, "The Ideal and Life"
("Das Ideal und das Leben"). Its original title was
"The Realm of Shadows ;" and this well expresses its
governing conception, which is, that we may, if we will,
escape from the narrow limits of daily existence into an
invisible world, peopled by beautiful forms, where duty
is merged in inclination, and where man achieves his
destiny without conflict or suffering.[1]

> " Not from the strife itself to set thee free,
>   But more to nerve, doth Victory
>   Wave her rich garland from the ideal clime.
>   Whate'er thy wish, the earth has no repose ;
>   Life still must drag thee onward as it flows,
>   Whirling thee down the dancing surge of Time.
>   But when the courage sinks beneath the dull
>   Sense of its narrow limits—on the soul,
>   Bright from the hill-tops of the Beautiful,
>   Bursts the attainèd goal !

[1] The poetical translations in this chapter are taken from the late
Lord Lytton's rendering of ' The Poems and Ballads of Schiller.'

If worth thy while the glory and the strife
Which fire the lists of actual life—
    The ardent rush to fortune or to fame,
In the hot field where strength and valour are,
And rolls the whirling thunder of the car,
    And the world, breathless, eyes the glorious game—
Then dare and strive—the prize can but belong
    To him whose valour o'er his tribe prevails;
In life, the victory only crowns the strong—
    He who is feeble fails.

But Life, whose source, by crags around it piled,
    Chafed while confined, foams fierce and wild,
Glides soft and smooth when once its streams expand,
When its waves, glassing in their silver play,
Aurora blent with Hesper's milder ray,
    Gain the still Beautiful—that shadow-land!
Here, contest grows but interchange of love,
    All curb is but the bondage of the Grace;
Gone is each foe,—Peace folds her wings above
    Her native dwelling-place."

At the close of the poem (which consists of fifteen
stanzas), Schiller presents the destiny of Hercules as a
figure of man's passage from the actual to an ideal
world :—

    " So, in the glorious parable, behold
    How, bowed to mortal bonds, of old
        Life's dreary path divine Alcides trod:
    The hydra and the lion were his prey,
    And to restore the friend he loved to-day,
        He went undaunted to the black-browed god;
    And all the torments and the labours sore
        Wroth Juno sent—the meek majestic One,
    With patient spirit and unquailing, bore,
        Until the course was run—

Until the god cast down his garb of clay,
And rent in hallowing flame away
　The mortal part from the divine—to soar
To the empyreal air !　Behold him spring
Blithe in the pride of the unwonted wing,
　And the dull matter that confined before
Sinks downward, downward, downward as a dream!
　Olympian hymns receive the escaping soul,
And smiling Hebe, from the ambrosial stream,
　Fills for a god the bowl ! "

Another poem, " Ideals " (" Die Ideale "), is a lament
that in mature life we leave so far behind us the impulses of nature, with the dreams and hopes of youth.
Its spirit is expressed in the following stanzas :—

" As once, with tearful passion fired,
　The Cyprian sculptor clasped the stone,
Till the cold cheeks, delight inspired,
　Blushed—to sweet life the marble grown :
So youth's desire for Nature !—round
　The Statue, so my arms I wreathed,
Till warmth and life in mine it found,
　And breath that poets breathe—it breathed ;

With my own burning thoughts it burned ;
　Its silence stirred to speech divine ;
Its lips my glowing kiss returned ;
　Its heart in beating answered mine !
How fair was then the flower—the tree !
　How silver-sweet the fountain's fall !
The soulless had a soul to me !
　My life its own life lent to all !

The Universe of Things seemed swelling
　The panting heart to burst its bound ;
And wandering Fancy found a dwelling
　In every shape, thought, deed, and sound.

> Germed in the mystic buds, reposing,
>   A whole creation slumbered mute;
> Alas, when from the buds unclosing,
>   How scant and blighted sprang the fruit!"

Wilhelm von Humboldt complained that the feeling
in this poem is not sufficiently generalised; but the
fact that it seems to spring directly from the heart
of the poet gives it a power which does not belong to
some of his more finished compositions; and it is sig-
nificant that Goethe considered it superior to any of
Schiller's previous lyrics. "The Walk" ("Der Spa-
ziergang") appeared at first simply as "An Elegy;"
and it was meant to be a study in one of the kinds
which Schiller had defined in 'Naïve and Sentimental
Poetry.' The poet leaves his room to enjoy the free
life of nature, and as he walks reflects on the peaceful
lot of the rural population, the complex life of cities,
the inequalities of society; and finally he takes refuge
from the insincerities and conventions of civilisation
in the living scenes of the outward world, "where the
sun of Homer still smiles on us." The same contrast
reappears in "Genius" ("Der Genius"); but here the
"nature" which he celebrates is that which asserts itself
in persons of strong and sincere character. All these,
and many other poems of this year, bear the stamp of
Schiller's moral ideal—the ideal of a mind which expresses itself in the grace and dignity of a perfect body;
which finds freedom in the highest laws of its being;
which, although ever exercising its powers, enjoys eternal
calm; and which is surrounded by, and has the faculty
of appreciating, beauty in an infinite variety of manifestations. He strikes an occasional note of sadness when

he remembers how far off this ideal is; but more frequently he rejoices in the conviction that, whatever may
be the poverty and meanness of reality, it is idealism
that discloses the true home of the human spirit.

The historical background to Schiller's activity at this
period is the war in which revolutionary France bade
defiance to nearly all Europe. Early in 1796 the scene
of conflict was transferred from the Rhine country and
the Netherlands to South Germany; and Schiller had
good reason to dread the possible consequences in the
quiet home at the Solitude. A very happy home it was;
and happiest of all in the little circle was his youngest
sister Nanette, who was looking forward with delight
to the opening of what she hoped would be a brilliant
career in the Weimar theatre. Suddenly Schiller learned
that she had been struck down by fever, which had
spread over the country from the Austrian hospital. He
anxiously awaited tidings; and in a few days came a
letter from his father announcing her death. The old
man himself was dangerously ill, and Louise had also
been attacked by the malady which had proved fatal to
her sister. Schiller would have started at once for Würtemberg, but the state of his health did not permit him
to travel; he accordingly wrote to his sister Christophine,
enclosing money, and begging her to go to their mother's
help. Thanks to Christophine's care, Louise recovered;
but their father soon followed Nanette, whose death had
broken his heart. Schiller at once offered his mother a
home in his house, but she preferred to remain near the
old scenes with her daughter Louise.

Sad as this year was, it was not all dark. Schiller
spent nearly a month with Goethe, who strove with the

utmost tenderness to cheer and console his friend. After
his return from Weimar he had the pleasure of welcom-
ing Körner and his family ; and as Goethe also came to
Jena, the three friends (for Körner had long known
Goethe) had much animating talk. The year was made
further memorable by the birth of Schiller's second son.
" Now," he wrote to Goethe, " I can begin to count my
small family. It is a peculiar feeling, and the step from
one to two is greater than I thought."

During this year (1796) Schiller chiefly occupied his
leisure with a kind of poetry to which he had not hitherto
given much attention—the epigrammatic. The ' Horen '
had been attacked in many periodicals, and he often
thought of retorting on his critics. Goethe advised him
to put all their criticisms together at the end of the year,
and dispose of them in a single article. " When things
of that kind," he wrote, " are made up in a bundle, they
burn better." In the course of conversation it occurred
to one of them that a good method of revenge would be
to make their assailants the subject of a series of epigrams, each to consist of a distich. The more they
thought of this suggestion the more they liked it, and
it quickly assumed larger proportions than they originally intended. So many writers of the day were dull,
or commonplace, or pretentious, that the opportunity
seemed an excellent one for asserting against them the
claims of true literature ; and it was at last decided to
print in the ' Almanac ' as many epigrams as could be
prepared in time, with the general title " Xenien "
(" Xenia," hospitable gifts, a title borrowed from Mar-
tial). The work was begun in common towards the
end of 1795 ; and as Goethe happened to be in Jena

for a fortnight early in 1796, they were able to carry
it on night after night without interruption. Afterwards they sent each other "Xenien" by the dozen,
and both anticipated with mischievous delight the alarm
which would be spread in the camp of the enemy by
so novel and unexpected an onslaught. Upwards of
four hundred of these epigrams were printed, and the
authorship of some of them is still uncertain. As a rule,
the most severe are Schiller's, but the majority were to
a large extent the work of both poets. Occasionally
the idea was suggested by one and executed by the
other, and in some instances each contributed a line.
Hardly one in the series deserves to be called a masterpiece of wit, but few are without force, brightness, and
edge. Here and there a great name occurs, and usually
with honour. To Lessing, for instance, a splendid epigram is dedicated, with the title "To Achilles;" and
Kant appears as a king who builds, while his expositors
are hodmen to whom his building gives employment.
For the most part the tone is one of biting sarcasm.
Few contemporary writers were spared—even Wieland
being made to figure as "the elegant young lady of
Weimar." Friedrich Stolberg and Lavater, although
friends of Goethe, had to listen to some plain words—
the latter for the charlatanism which mingled with his
better qualities, the former for his narrow pietism.
The hottest fire of all was directed against poor old
Nicolai, the Berlin bookseller, who, having begun life
as the friend of Lessing and Mendelssohn, fancied that
he was a valiant champion of enlightenment and toler-
ation, but saw himself here in the foremost ranks of the
Philistines. Loud and prolonged was the outcry raised

by the sufferers, and even by some who had not suffered,
but who could not tell what might yet be in store for
them.   Herder (whose name had not occurred) fiercely
denounced the poets, and Nicolai called the 'Almanac'
an "Almanac of the Furies."   Innumerable "Anti-
Xenien" were published, and Schiller, had not Goethe
dissuaded him, would have prepared a new assault.
Goethe watched the storm calmly, and was not displeased by it; and the opinion he expressed to Schiller
was, that they should now devote themselves to "greater
and worthier works," and "put their enemies to shame
by changing their Protean nature into forms of the
noble and the good."

Many epigrams of a more serious nature were produced
at the same time as the "Xenien."   Of these the best
were the "Votivtafeln" ("Tabulæ Votivæ"), each epigram
expressing some truth which had helped the poet in life,
and which in gratitude he piously hung up as a "tabula
votiva" in the sanctuary.   So it is explained in the introductory distich.   These epigrams are in their own way
as fine as any of the writings which were the direct fruit
of Schiller's philosophical meditations.   The thought
expressed in all of them is marked by his ideal tone, and
the form is so compressed and precise that they bring
us into contact with the essence of his governing principles.   Some admirable lyrics also belong to the same
year.   In "Pompeii and Herculaneum" we find ourselves in a realm of fancy altogether different from any
in which Schiller has hitherto presented himself.   Here
there are no moral reflections; he simply pictures the
streets of the disinterred cities as if they were still the
busy scenes of ancient life, and the figures start forth

with remarkable force and vividness. "The Maid from
other Lands" ("Das Mädchen aus der Fremde") is an
allegorical lyric, in which, with exquisite grace and simplicity, he celebrates the power and the loveliness of
poetry. Another allegory, "The Lament of Ceres"
("Die Klage der Ceres"), has brilliant rhetorical passages ; but critics have never been able to agree as to
its hidden significance. A happier effort is "Dithy-
ramb" ("Dithyrambe"), originally entitled "The Visit"
(meaning a visit of the gods), in which, under the figure
of one to whom Bacchus has given rapturous visions,
Schiller describes the poet in an hour of exaltation and
inspiration.

In 1797 Schiller's health was so bad that for several
months he could not go out of doors. A great longing
for the country seized him, and fortunately a garden-
house which was exactly to his taste happened at this
time to become vacant. This he bought, and he and
his family took possession of it in May. It was situated
on the slope of a hill near Jena, and commanded splendid
views of the valley of the Saale. At the upper end of
the large garden Schiller erected a hut in which he spent
the summer days at work ; and beside it was a bower,
where there is still the old stone table at which he and
Goethe (as Goethe long afterwards said when revisiting
the spot) "exchanged many a good and great word."
Before going to this delightful retreat he had spent many
pleasant evenings with Goethe, who had been in Jena for
more than a month. Wilhelm von Humboldt, who after a
long absence had returned, always joined them ; and Schiller was still further cheered by the society of Wilhelm von
Wolzogen and Caroline, who were now married, and had

been living for some time in Jena. In spring, however, Humboldt went away, and the Wolzogens changed their residence to Weimar. Goethe, too, was planning a long tour in Switzerland. Much as Schiller enjoyed his country-house and garden, he sadly missed his friends, and he looked forward with positive sorrow to the prospect of Goethe's absence.

"Hermann and Dorothea," which the world owes chiefly to the impetus communicated to Goethe by Schiller, was finished about this time, and Schiller read it again and again. "Your Hermann," he wrote, "leads me, merely through its pure poetic form, into a divine world of poetry, while your 'Wilhelm Meister' scarcely lets me escape from a real world." Inspired by Goethe's example, and by the influences of nature, Schiller laboured joyfully in his garden-house for the next number of the 'Almanac;' and fortunately he had found a kind of work in which there was perfect scope for his energies. He and Goethe had talked much lately of ballad literature, which had been made as popular by Herder in Germany as by Percy in England; and they agreed to write a number of ballads simultaneously, submitting their work to each other as they advanced. Schiller entered into the scheme with zest, and in the course of a few months produced six ballads, which rank among his highest achievements. Any one who goes through Schiller's works in the order in which they were written, comes with surprise and delight upon these beautiful poems. In "Pompeii and Herculaneum" he had given some indication of what he could do if he chose simply to represent objects; but in his ballads he far surpasses even that vivid picture. He limits him-

self absolutely to the scenes in which he desires to
interest us, and he makes them visible by images of
extraordinary variety, definiteness, and vivacity.

The earliest of Schiller's ballads was "The Diver"
("Der Taucher"), in which he gave splendid form to an
ancient legend. The king, his daughter, his knights
and squires, stand at the edge of a rugged cliff over-
hanging the sea, and look down on a raging whirlpool.
In the opening stanza the king cries—

> "Oh, where is the knight or the squire so bold,
>   As to dive to the howling Charybdis below ?—
> I cast in the whirlpool a goblet of gold,
>   And o'er it already the dark waters flow ;
> Whoever to me may the goblet bring,
> Shall have for his guerdon that gift of his king."

Thrice he repeats his question, but no one answers, until
at last a youthful squire, "gentle and bold," moves forward and casts aside his girdle and mantle. Amid the
wonder of the courtiers, he gazes steadily down into the
gulf.

> " As he strode to the marge of the summit, and gave
>   One glance on the gulf of that merciless main ;
> Lo ! the wave that for ever devours the wave,
>   Casts roaringly up the Charybdis again ;
> And, as with the swell of the far thunder-boom,
> Rushes foamingly forth from the heart of the gloom.
>
> And it bubbles and seethes, and it hisses and roars,
>   As when fire is with water commixed and contending,
> And the spray of its wrath to the welkin upsoars,
>   And flood upon flood hurries on, never ending.
> And it never *will* rest, nor from travail be free,
> Like a sea that is labouring the birth of a sea."

At last the rage is allayed, and amid the foam yawns a dark chasm, into which the surging billows are swept.

"The youth gave his trust to his Maker! Before
    That path through the riven abyss closed again—
Hark! a shriek from the crowd rang aloft from the shore,
    And, behold! he is whirled in the grasp of the main!
And o'er him the breakers mysteriously rolled,
And the giant-mouth closed on the swimmer so bold."

An interval of dreadful suspense follows, during which the hollow roar of the waters below the surface becomes more and more terrible; and soon the waves begin to sweep upwards with their former fury.

"And, lo! from the heart of that far-floating gloom,
    What gleams on the darkness so swan-like and white?
Lo! an arm and a neck, glancing up from the tomb!—
    They battle—the Man's with the Element's might.
It is he—it is he!—in his left hand behold,
As a sign—as a joy!—shines the goblet of gold!"

The king's daughter fills the goblet with wine, and the youth describes his adventure.

"'Happy they whom the rose-hues of daylight rejoice,
    The air and the sky that to mortals are given!
May the horror below never more find a voice—
    Nor Man stretch too far the wide mercy of Heaven!
Never more—never more may he lift from the sight
The veil which is woven with Terror and Night!

'Quick-brightening like lightning—it tore me along,
    Down, down, till the gush of a torrent at play,
In the rocks of its wilderness, caught me—and strong
    As the wings of an eagle, it whirled me away.
Vain, vain was my struggle—the circle had won me,
Round and round in its dance, the wild element spun me.

'And I called on my God, and my God heard my prayer,
  In the strength of my need, in the gasp of my breath—
And showed me a crag that rose up from the lair,
  And I clung to it nimbly—and baffled the death!
And, safe in the perils around me, behold
On the spikes of the coral the goblet of gold.

'Below, at the foot of that precipice drear,
  Spread the gloomy, and purple, and pathless Obscure!
A silence of horror that slept on the ear,
  That the eye more appalled might the horror endure!
Salamander—snake—dragon—vast reptiles that dwell
In the deep—coiled about the grim jaws of their hell.

'Dark-crawled—glided dark the unspeakable swarms,
  Clumped together in masses, misshapen and vast—
Here clung and here bristled the fashionless forms—
  Here the dark-moving bulk of the hammer-fish passed—
And with teeth grinning white, and a menacing motion,
Went the terrible shark—the hyæna of ocean.

'There I hung, and the awe gathered icily o'er me,
  So far from the earth, where man's help there was none!
The one human thing, with the goblins before me—
  Alone—in a loneness so ghastly—alone!
Fathom-deep from man's eye in the speechless profound,
With the death of the main and the monsters around.

'Methought, as I gazed through the darkness, that now
  It saw—the dread hundred-limbed creature—its prey!
And darted—O God! from the far-flaming bough
  Of the coral, I swept on the horrible way;
And it seized me, the wave with its wrath and its roar,
It seized me to save—King, the danger is o'er!'"

Longing for fresh excitement, the king proposes that the
youth shall dive into the whirlpool for a ring and bring

tidings of what he sees " in the nethermost ground of
the sea."

" Then out spake the daughter in tender emotion :
    ' Ah, father, my father, what more can there rest ?
Enough of this sport with the pitiless ocean—
    He has served thee as none would, thyself hast confest.
If nothing can slake thy wild thirst of desire,
Let thy knights put to shame the exploit of the squire ! '

The king seized the goblet—he swung it on high,
    And whirling, it fell in the roar of the tide :
' But bring back that goblet again to my eye,
    And I'll hold thee the dearest that rides by my side ;
And thine arms shall embrace, as thy bride, I decree,
The maiden whose pity now pleadeth for thee.'

In his heart, as he listened, there leapt the wild joy—
    And the hope and the love through his eyes spoke in fire,
On that bloom, on that blush, gazed delighted the boy ;
    The maiden—she faints at the feet of her sire !
Here the guerdon divine, there the danger beneath ;
He resolves !—To the strife with the life and the death !

They hear the loud surges sweep back in their swell,
    Their coming the thunder-sound heralds along !
Fond eyes yet are tracking the spot where he fell :
    They come, the wild waters, in tumult and throng,
Roaring up to the cliff—roaring back, as before,
But no wave ever brings the lost youth to the shore."

In this fine poem there is no pause in the interest, and
emotion is touched at almost every point where it is
capable of intense expression. Schiller's only direct
knowledge of the appearance of whirlpools was derived
from observation of a mill-stream ; but the impressions
obtained in this humble manner were so truly combined

and so splendidly vivified, that Goethe found every trait marked in the poem reproduced at the Falls of Schaffhausen.

A worthy pendant to " The Diver " was " The Glove " (" Der Handschuh "), in which, with equal animation, Schiller shows us a knight descending for his lady's glove into an arena occupied by wild beasts ; and afterwards, when she is prepared to welcome him with smiles, refusing her thanks and bidding her an abrupt farewell. The theme of " The Ring of Polycrates " (" Der Ring des Polykrates ") is the ancient dread of the jealousy with which the gods were supposed to watch an excess of human happiness ; and this sentiment is brought home to us by many quick transitions of scene and feeling. In " Knight Toggenburg " (" Ritter Toggenburg "), the hero of which fights valiantly in the Holy Land, and on his return, finding that his lady has entered a convent, becomes a hermit, there is the same truth of perception ; but its tone, being more sentimental, is less impressive than that of the other ballads. Schiller made ample amends by " The Cranes of Ibycus " (" Die Kraniche des Ibykus "), in completing which he was indebted for valuable suggestions to Goethe, who also thought of dealing with the subject, but abandoned his purpose on reading Schiller's poem. Ibycus, the light-hearted poet, fares on to the Olympian games ; but on his way he is murdered in a wood by two robbers, and as he is dying he looks up and sees a flock of cranes, to which he cries to be his avengers. We are introduced into a theatre crowded by an eager throng ; we hear the fearful song of the Furies ; at its close a shadow passes across the theatre, for a flock of cranes is flying over-

head ; and the stillness is broken by a voice from one
of the highest tiers, " See, see, Timotheus, the cranes of
Ibycus ! " And thus the murderers are revealed and
dragged to justice. This is one of the most imaginative
of Schiller's poems : it fills us with a consciousness
of the mysterious influences of destiny ; yet we are
immediately confronted only by ordinary facts of nature,
and by familiar promptings of human feeling. The last
of this series was " The Walk to the Forge " ("Der
Gang nach dem Eisenhammer "). Here Schiller abandons his dramatic manner, and presents the incidents
in the flowing style of an epic narrative ; and he is as
happy in the one method as in the other. Fridolin, a
youth in the service of the Countess Savern, wins by his
fidelity her confidence and goodwill. Robert, the envious huntsman, excites the jealousy of her lord, who
conceives a dreadful revenge. Two men working at the
forge are directed to cast into the furnace the messenger
who shall come from him with the question, " How have
you fulfilled the master's order ? " Fridolin is despatched with the message, but on the way, in obedience
to his mistress, enters the church to pray for her sick
child. He is delayed by the priest, and on reaching the
forge is told by the men with a grim smile that the
master's will has been done. The fate destined for him
had overtaken his enemy ; and the Count, seeing that
" God Himself had judged," conducts the youth to the
Countess, and acknowledges that he deserves her favour.
So wild a tale would have been made ridiculous by a
single false note ; but Schiller escapes this peril by perfect grace and simplicity. In two ballads written in

the following year (1798) — "The Conflict with the Dragon" ("Der Kampf mit dem Drachen"), and "Security" ("Bürgschaft")—he returned to the dramatic style, and with no decay of power. The latter is a glowing picture of ancient friendship. Damon, condemned to be crucified by Dionysius, the tyrant of Syracuse, begs for three days' grace, that he may be present at his sister's wedding; and his friend, Phintias, becomes security for him. Schiller has hardly anywhere displayed more vigour than in his description of the agony with which, after the wedding, the condemned man struggles with various obstacles that threaten to make him too late to deliver his friend from peril. In "The Conflict with the Dragon" we do not see the fight while it is in progress,—we only hear the conqueror's report of it; but his deed is thus made more impressive, since we perceive the effect it produces on the crowd whom he addresses. He is a knight; and the master of his Order, while recognising his bravery, decrees that he shall be dismissed for undertaking an adventure which had been forbidden. Schiller contrasts admirably the knight's valour with the spirit of humble submission by which he at last overcomes his superior's displeasure.

While Schiller was occupied with his ballads, he did not forget other forms of poetry. During this time he wrote at least one lyric, "Expectation" ("Die Erwartung"), which ranks among the best love-poems in German literature. It is a lover who speaks; he is waiting for "her" in the twilight, and every moment he persuades himself that she is approaching :—

" Hear I the creaking gate unclose ?
  The gleaming latch uplifted ?
No—'twas the wind that, whirring, rose,
  Amidst the poplars drifted !

Adorn thyself, thou green leaf-bowering roof,
  Destined the bright one's presence to receive,
For her, a shadowy palace-hall aloof
  With holy Night, thy boughs familiar weave.
And ye sweet flatteries of the delicate air,
  Awake and sport her rosy cheek around,
When their light weight the tender feet shall bear,
  When Beauty comes to Passion's trysting-ground.

Hush ! what amidst the copses crept—
  So swiftly by me now ?
No,—'twas the startled bird that swept
  The light leaves of the bough !

Day, quench thy torch ! come, ghost-like, from on high,
  With thy loved Silence, come, thou haunting Eve !
Broaden below thy web of purple dye,
  Which lullèd boughs mysterious round us weave.
For love's delight, enduring listeners none,
  The froward witness of the light will flee ;
Hesper alone, the rosy Silent One,
  Down-glancing may our sweet Familiar be !

.   .   .   .

What yonder seems to glimmer ?
  Her white robe's glancing hues ?—
No,—'twas the column's shimmer
  Athwart the darksome yews !

Oh, longing heart, no more delight-upbuoyed,
  Let the sweet airy image thee befool !
The arms that would embrace her clasp the void :
  This feverish breast no phantom-bliss can cool.

Oh, waft her here, the *true*, the *living* one !
  Let but my hand *her* hand, the tender, feel—
The very shadow of her robe alone !—
  So into life the idle dream shall steal!

As glide from heaven, when least we ween,
  The rosy hours of bliss,
All gently came the maid, unseen :—
  He waked beneath her kiss !"

There are several other lyrics of the same class—"To
Emma" ("An Emma"), "The Meeting" ("Die Begeg-
nung"), and "The Secret" ("Das Geheimniss")—all
of them finely conceived, but without the life that glows
in "Expectation." In "Happiness" ("Das Glück"),
Schiller returns to his earlier manner, enforcing with
great power the idea that happiness is not to be attained
by effort, but is a gift of the gods, and that "a sublime, a divine lot" awaits those who are born with a
calm and joyful mind. It is supposed that Schiller was
thinking of Goethe when he wrote this poem, and the
opening verses have been placed on the pedestal of
Goethe's bust in the Weimar Library. "The Eleusinian
Festival" ("Das Eleusische Fest") is in the form of a
hymn for the Eleusinian Mysteries,—a song of praise
dedicated to Ceres, the founder of civil life. It has
some resemblance in the order of its ideas to "The
Walk," where Schiller reviews some of the characteristics of human society. Here he follows in regular grad-
ation the advance of man from the hunting to the nomadic stage, from the nomadic stage to the growth of agriculture, and so to all the varied phases of civilisation,
celebrating each stage in verses of lofty rhetoric.

Greater than all these poems—greater even than the

ballads—is "The Song of the Bell" ("Das Lied von der Glocke"), which belongs to this period. The conception of "The Song" had been for a long time in Schiller's mind. Even during his first residence in Volkstädt he used to visit a foundry in Rudolstadt, for the purpose of making himself familiar with the process of casting bells. He worked at the scheme at many different times, but was unable to give it its final form until 1799. Next to his greatest dramas, this is the poem by which Schiller is best known; and it fully deserves the rank which is commonly attributed to it. In some respects it has an affinity to "The Walk" and "The Eleusinian Festival," for, like them, its aim is to present a picture of human life; but its range is wider, and the means by which its end is accomplished are incomparably more artistic. The dominating element is formed by the casting of the bell. This is not merely described; we see the process from first to last, the master of the foundry (who is supposed to speak throughout) marking the successive stages in a series of bold and graphic verses. All is stir, movement, animation; and each word strikes so swiftly and vigorously, that a multitude of associations start into consciousness, and combine to form a living image of the scene. First we see the mould in the earth; then the furnace is fed by masses of wood; the metal is melted and tested; it is poured into the mould; there is a pause while it cools; the mould is broken; the bell is disclosed, bright and smooth; and finally it is raised from its bed in the soil, to be afterwards elevated to "the realm of sound in the air of heaven." Between each stanza the master pictures some typical aspect of life, varying his metre in

accordance with the thought or the sentiment which he
wishes to express, and connecting his descriptions with
the uses to which a public bell is applied. He begins
with the child's birth, and advances through boyhood to
the days of hope and love. Then come marriage and
mature life,—the father struggling with the world for his
children ; the mother ruling her house with wisdom, tenderness, and diligence. But the ringing of the bell pro-
claims two calamities,—the destruction of their house by
fire, and the mother's death. At this point the metal
has been poured into the mould ; and while it cools the
master gives his thoughts a wider sweep, contrasting the
plenty and the happiness which spring from public order
and peace with the disasters caused by revolutionary
rage. These images and reflections would have been of
too varied a nature to be combined in a single work
without the central action ; but from this they derive
the kind of unity which is sometimes given to a landscape by a beautiful stream winding through it. In
"The Song of the Bell," all the highest powers of
Schiller move in harmony. It presents both dramatic
and lyrical elements ; and while it contains deep and
serious thought, its thought does not appeal to us directly
through the understanding, but indirectly through imagination and feeling.

During these years, notwithstanding his pressing en-
gagements, Schiller had never lost sight of the drama : it
was his firm intention to make it the leading object of
his life. Fortunately, when he began to think seriously
of returning to it, he had not to cast about for a theme ;
for we have seen that, while at Carlsbad in 1791, he
was already devising a play of which Wallenstein was

to be the hero. Ill health, philosophical study, and the need of making money, prevented him from advancing with it rapidly; but he often jotted down suggestions as they occurred to him, especially during his visit to Swabia, and in 1796 he carefully brought these together in the hope of making a fresh start. In 1797 he wrote a rhymed prelude, and began the body of the play, composing it at first in prose, but afterwards deciding to present it in rhythmic form. When once fairly on his path, he found that the chief difficulty arose from the wealth of his material; and he was soon forced to pause, to consider by what means he might hope to bring it within the compass of a single play. In September 1798 he spent a week in Weimar; and after much consultation with Goethe, to whom he read what he had written, he at last saw his way clear. The Prelude he would extend to the proportions of an independent work; and the tragedy itself he would divide into two parts—" The Piccolomini " (" Die Piccolomini ") and " Wallenstein's Death " (" Wallensteins Tod "). At this time the Weimar theatre was undergoing extensive repairs, and it was agreed between Goethe and Schiller that it should be reopened on the 12th of October 1798 with the Prelude, " Wallenstein's Camp " (" Wallensteins Lager ").

In the solitude of his garden-house Schiller laboured incessantly at his scheme, and he was able to send the manuscript to Goethe in good time. Goethe, however, had now to see Schiller in a new aspect. Every day improvements suggested themselves; and while the actors were studying their parts, messengers constantly arrived from Jena with unexpected directions. All was taken

in good part by the imperturbable Goethe, who exerted
himself to the utmost to gratify his friend's wishes;
and on the appointed day the Prelude was represented.
Its reception was even more cordial than the poet had
ventured to anticipate, so that he returned to "The
Piccolomini" with heightened courage.   He was in
wretched health; but weariness and pain were not
allowed to interrupt his work.   Before the end of
1798 he despatched the play to Berlin, where Iffland, the
director of the Royal Theatre, was impatiently waiting
for it; and soon afterwards, with many changes for the
better, it was in Goethe's hands.   In order to superin-
tend the rehearsals with Goethe, he went to Weimar for
almost a month in the beginning of 1799, and during
this visit the two friends approached each other more
closely than ever.   On the 30th of January 1799,
"The Piccolomini" was played for the first time; and
although the public did not seem to realise its importance,
it was welcomed with enthusiasm by all for whose judgment Schiller had high respect.   On the second representation, a night or two afterwards, spectators of all
classes were impressed by its great conceptions and noble
style.   Among those who heartily congratulated him
was the Duke of Weimar; and he also received a letter of warm appreciation from his old friend, Charlotte
von Kalb, to whom he replied that he was glad *she*
had "found" him in the play, for in it he had expressed
"his being."

"The Piccolomini" in its original form included the
first two acts of what is now "Wallenstein's Death."
What remained to be done, therefore, he could hope to
accomplish rapidly; and about the middle of March

1799, Goethe had in his possession the complete work. In April all three pieces were represented, a night being given to each; and, seen thus as parts of one scheme, they excited almost universal admiration. Christophine, who followed with pride the triumphant progress of her brother's career, learned from Lotte that "everybody in the theatre had sobbed, and that even the actors cried;" and Schiller himself wrote to Körner that the impression had been "extraordinary," and that "during the following eight days nothing else had been talked about." Soon afterwards the work was again represented in Weimar, for the pleasure of Frederick William III. of Prussia and Queen Louise (the parents of the Emperor William), and the beautiful queen had many pleasant things to say to the poet. The Duchess of Weimar was equally gracious, and in testimony of her appreciation sent Lotte a present of a silver coffee-service. Schiller was much pleased by this recognition, and laughingly observed that "poets should always be rewarded by presents, not paid, for there was a certain relationship between fortunate gifts and gifts of fortune" ("zwischen den glücklichen Gaben und den Gaben des Glücks") —"both fell from heaven."

For several years he had often thought of transferring his residence from Jena to Weimar, and the wish was strengthened in proportion as he occupied himself with the drama. In Weimar he would have the advantage of being in direct contact with the stage, whereas in Jena there was no kind of influence to stimulate and correct his dramatic genius. Besides, he would be near Goethe; and both he and Lotte would find it agreeable to live in the same town with her sister Caroline. The only difficulty was that in Weimar his expenses would be increased. This was a formidable obstacle, for the 'Horen' and the 'Musenalmanach,' having become excessively burdensome, had both been given up (the former in 1798, the latter in 1799); and although he had been made, in 1798, a full professor (Professor Ordinarius), this honour had not been accompanied by any addition to his small salary of 200 thalers. He accordingly wrote to the Duke, applying for an increase of salary, and stating his reasons. The Duke replied in a friendly spirit, offering to double the amount. As Schiller had already received what he considered handsome pay for "Wallenstein," and as he hoped that his future works would be equally well rewarded, he concluded that the proposed change might now be safely made; and on the 3d of December 1799, he and his family left Jena and established themselves in Weimar.

CHAPTER XI.

"WALLENSTEIN" is often spoken of as a trilogy; but if it is meant that Schiller copied the model of the Greek trilogy, the term is misleading. In a Greek trilogy each member of the group, while having relations to the rest, forms an independent work of art. No part of "Wallenstein" is fully intelligible without reference to the intention of the whole; and as we have seen, Schiller divided the work into three plays merely because a single drama did not seem to provide verge enough for the mass of his conceptions.

The nearest approach to independence is made by the Prelude, "Wallenstein's Camp," where we are presented with a picture of the military circumstances in which the action unfolds itself. This is one of the most energetic and lifelike representations that we owe to Schiller's genius. It places us in the midst of the Thirty Years' War, and reveals the precise character of the instruments wielded by the struggling jealousies and ambitions of that tempestuous era. By a few bold strokes we are reminded of the agitated and suffering world beyond the limits of Wallenstein's headquarters. The starving peasant with his timid boy, the citizen pleading with his son not to join the army, the rough parson who denounces the wickedness of the soldier's life, each in his own way makes visible to us the desolating effects of the war on the different classes of society. We remain, however, within the camp; and all its varied elements are disclosed by a number of typical figures who represent the aims, the ideas, and the passions of their comrades. Dugald Dalgetty has made English readers familiar with the kind of soldier of fortune who emerged from the Thirty Years' War, and the characters in "Wallenstein's Camp" have all his contempt for danger and his indifference to the principles at stake in the conflict into which he throws himself. They are conceived, however, — although not with greater vividness,—in a more poetic spirit. They love the life of wild adventure, and fight not merely for gain, but because the excitement of battle stirs the blood. And for the time they are united in a firm and compact mass, for whatever may be the differences in their objects and their hopes, they are agreed in a passionate devotion to their commander. Wallenstein does not personally appear in the Prelude, but in all its scenes we feel the influence of his mighty spirit. This common feeling gives unity to the play, and evokes in the spectator a mood which is favourable to the parts that follow. Curiosity is awakened, and we are prepared for the manifestation of a strange and potent genius.

In "The Piccolomini" Wallenstein passes before us, but without revealing his essential qualities : the foreground is occupied by his great officers. Here again he exercises an indirect influence on the imagination,

for he engages all minds ; he is the theme of incessant
discussion; the hopes and fears of the characters vary
in the measure of their repugnance to, or their sympathy
with, his daring plans. At last, in " Wallenstein's
Death," he steps forth with all the force of his commanding nature; he fills the stage, and to the end the
interest is centred in his slowly approaching doom.

Wallenstein was murdered early in 1634. About
eighteen months before, he had fought the battle of
Lützen, in which Gustavus Adolphus fell; and almost
immediately afterwards he began to excite the sus-
picion of the Imperial Court by his dilatory and uncertain movements. He was found to be intriguing
with the enemy, and the Emperor Ferdinand, afraid to
proceed openly against so powerful a foe, issued a secret
order deposing him from the command, and plainly in-
timating a wish that his life should be taken. Wallenstein's aims cannot be exactly determined; but it is at
least known that he desired to secure the crown of
Bohemia, and to grasp powers which would enable him
to determine the issues of the war in accordance with
his own opinions and interests. Schiller remains faithful to the broad facts of the history ; but in his presentation of Wallenstein's character he gives free scope to
his creative power. Of all his dramatic figures this is
the one in which he touches life at the greatest number
of points. The element in Wallenstein, as Schiller conceives him, which first strikes the imagination, is his
loneliness. He stands in the midst of a moving world,
surrounded by men of force and passion; but he towers
above all, admitting no one to his confidence, and cherish-
ing schemes which, if accomplished, must alter the course

of human progress. Yet in his manner there is nothing strained or theatrical. He speaks with ease and simplicity, and knows how to attach subordinates by a graceful and kindly bearing. And there are touches which show that, if he has an unlimited ambition, he is not without tender feeling. His daughter, Thecla, he sincerely loves; and for Max Piccolomini he has a warm and undying affection. These, however, are elements of minor importance; what absorbs attention is his passion for greatness, and his dark resolve to achieve it. It is sometimes said that Schiller tries to soften the repugnance with which we contemplate Wallenstein's crime by the fact that he does not at once succumb to temptation. But he passes through no genuine conflict. True, he wavers, argues with himself, dwells on the difficulties of his adventure, even recalls his obligations to the sovereign against whom he proposes to rebel; but we know that, whether or not he himself is fully aware of it, he has formed his decision long before he openly executes it. Before the beginning of the action in the drama he sends for his wife and daughter; he despatches to the Swedish camp letters and verbal messages which absolutely commit him; while he seems to hesitate, he directs Count Tertzky to obtain by any means, foul or fair, the signatures of his generals to a document pledging them unconditionally to his service; and when at last he is moved by the arguments of the Countess Tertzky, the fact that he gives way before her transparent sophisms proves that he has been convinced all along, and that his delays have been due merely to a temperament which, although delighting in vast schemes, shrinks from

delivering the final blow. In the great soliloquy before
his decisive interview with the Swedish ambassador he
is not consciously insincere; but we see, and Schiller
meant us to see, that his agitation is only on the surface, and plays over a deep and settled resolve.

But although Wallenstein does not really contend
against temptation, he is a true object of tragic pity.
First of all, his passion for greatness is not altogether
selfish; he fully believes that Germany is being ruined
by the unrelenting fanaticism of the Emperor, and that
he himself, if he becomes her master, will be able to
give her peace, order, and contentment. He intends to
begin his new career by joining the Swedes; but his
ultimate aim is to drive them and all invaders from the
fatherland. A still deeper impression is made upon us
by the fact that Wallenstein is subject to a mysterious
destiny. In one of Schiller's philosophical essays he
had expressed the opinion that the perfection of the
Greek drama is marred by the part which destiny plays
in it. Partly through a profounder study of Greek
literature, partly through the natural growth of his conception of the world, he had been led to abandon this
view; and in " Wallenstein " he makes destiny the con-
trolling principle which penetrates to the inmost recesses of its thought. Wallenstein has a passionate faith
in astrology, and sees his fate marked in unmistakable
characters in the stars. He has therefore no alternative
but to move towards the end to which he is called; he
is driven forward by a power to which, he thinks, the
human will can offer only a feeble and vain resistance.
If he had made energetic and skilful use of his opportunities, it is possible (so far as the forces introduced in

the play are concerned) that success would have been
within his reach. He is adored by the majority of the
army ; and the wavering minority might perhaps have
been won by a swift and brilliant stroke. But he takes
no precautions, and when his officers begin to desert
him, offers no serious resistance. He merely conducts
the remnant of his army from Pilsen to Eger, with the
intention of effecting a junction with the Swedes. Not
thus do Richard III. and Macbeth yield to circumstances : they fight to the last, and by their unresting
vigour excite a far deeper interest than the inactive
Wallenstein. We are not, however, surprised by his
inactivity, for he is lulled by the assurance that whether
he fights or not, his triumph is secure. Even an hour
before his murder, when the Countess Tertzky is overcome by sad forebodings, he is serene and confident; he
looks up into the dark and stormy sky, and sees the
glimmer of Cassiopeia, in which is Jupiter, the planet
of his nativity. But all the time, behind his false
destiny, true destiny is working. If his course is inevitable, not less inevitable is the action of the powers
which gradually close in upon and crush him. Deep as
the empire had sunk below its ancient splendour, it was
still too great to be shattered by one who would not
strain every nerve to destroy it. Since Wallenstein,
instead of acting, indolently trusted to the stars, it was
easy for the Emperor's agents to detach his friends, and
to weave around him meshes of intrigue from which
escape was impossible. Thus, when he falls, we feel
that we have been throughout confronted by Necessity
—in his ambition, in his betrayal of trust, in his inert-
ness, and in his ruin.

The principal agent of Wallenstein's fall is Octavio Piccolomini, who has remained loyal to the Emperor. He shows an exact knowledge of men, especially of their weaker qualities; and we are obliged to confess that his course is determined only by worthy motives. But he does not gain our esteem, as apparently Schiller desired that he should do; for Wallenstein, whose power he undermines, was the friend of his youth, has conferred upon him innumerable favours, and trusts him absolutely. The officers who surround Wallenstein are, without exception, drawn with a masterly hand. Among the most striking are Count Tertzky and Marshal Illo, who, as courageous as they are reckless, are always ready to foster Wallenstein's evil designs, and yet never possess the key to his real thoughts. In Tiefenbach we have an excellent example of the rough German soldier who maintains, even amid the revolutionary violence of the Thirty Years' War, the traditional reverence for ancient institutions; while Isolani, the General of the Croats, represents with equal force the adventurer who renders his service to those who offer him most pay. Butler, the Irish colonel of dragoons, who murders Wallenstein, is at first one of his warmest friends: but his friendship is turned to enmity by a supposed wrong; and there is admirable art in the manner in which he is made to persuade himself that he acts from a sense of public duty and by an impulse of fate, while the true power which moves him is a craving for revenge. Von Questenberg has the firmness and the polished manner which become an imperial ambassador; and Seni, the astrologer, preserves, without caricature, the air of mystery which belongs to his calling. The Duchess

of Friedland, Wallenstein's wife, is natural in all her
movements ; but her timid nature is thrust into the
background by his bold, unscrupulous sister, the Countess Tertzky, in whom there is evidently a reminiscence
of Lady Macbeth, although she lacks the grandeur of
Lady Macbeth's ambition.

All these characters are figures taken directly from
actual life : they are such characters as we might expect
to meet in their sphere in a confused and troubled age.
It was hard for Schiller to be thus limited to the unbend-
ing outlines of realistic forms, so he created an outlet for
his deepest impulses in two natures, who stand forth in
vivid contrast with the world to which they belong.
These are Max Piccolomini, son of Octavio Piccolomini,
and Thecla, Wallenstein's daughter. Max is young, energetic, a brilliant soldier, yet preferring the joys of peace
to the excitement of war. Wallenstein loves him as a
son, and for Wallenstein he has an unbounded reverence
and devotion. It is he who is sent to conduct the
Duchess and her daughter to the camp, and during their
journey his heart is filled with love for Thecla, who
responds to it with an ardour equal to his own. When
they arrive at headquarters, Thecla intuitively feels
that more serious events are in progress than any that
meet the eye, and that disaster is approaching. Max,
bold, light-hearted, and rejoicing in his love, is unconscious of peril, and thinks only of the means by which
he may be able to persuade Thecla's father to surrender
her. Octavio Piccolomini cautiously reveals to him
Wallenstein's designs, but Max rejects with anger any
imputation on his commander's honour : never will he
believe anything to the discredit of one so great, unless

he hears it from the lips of Wallenstein himself. At last Wallenstein takes the young officer into his confidence, and then begins in Max a tragic conflict which cleaves his heart in twain. Nothing in the play approaches the imaginative energy with which this conflict is pictured. To quit Wallenstein is to quit the man in whom, of all others, he has had the strongest faith; and it is to lose Thecla, without whom, as he thinks, life will be unrelieved suffering. How can he rise to such a sacrifice? Wallenstein pleads with him for the sake of old and dear memories, and strives to prove to him that duty does not summon him away. Max's simple and sincere nature, however, penetrates to the naked truth; and he feels that if his ideal is not to be for ever shattered, he must obey the inward voice which speaks to him in clear tones. In his agony he turns to Thecla, and asks her to decide. The struggle which agitates him agitates her in a like degree; but, cost what it may, she cannot do other than bid him follow the promptings of his own heart. And he goes forth, free and pure, but with pain too sharp to be borne, and finds almost immediate deliverance by death on the field. Thecla's heart, too, is broken; and we catch our last glimpse of her as she prepares to go and die upon his grave.

This tragedy within a tragedy is the highest tide-mark of Schiller's dramatic power. We are awed by the spectacle of destiny sweeping grandly forward to its goal, and crushing the forms which obstruct its path; but it fills us with a sense of our insignificance, and had the fate of Wallenstein alone been unrolled before us, the effect of the drama would have been only sad and depressing. A firmer note is struck by the ideal passions

of Max and Thecla. Even to what appears to be destiny
they do not yield, but gather their energies together and
dash themselves against it, knowing well that by death
alone they can save their spiritual integrity and freedom.
Thus the dominant mood produced by "Wallenstein"
is not one of mere resignation; we are also made vividly
conscious of human greatness. To Max and Thecla,
too, it is due that amid the clash of mighty forces a
lyrical note of exquisite sweetness breaks upon the ear,
for in a beautiful scene they open their hearts to each
other in all the confidence of perfect love. It is as
if, in a gathering storm, the black clouds parted for a
moment, and revealed the clear depths of the infinite
blue.

Schiller's chief plays have been translated into nearly
every European language, but "Wallenstein" had the
rare fortune to be rendered into English soon after its
publication by a great poet. Coleridge translated the
work in its earliest form (omitting the Prelude), and
allowed himself considerable liberties in his task, ampli-
fying some passages until they bore quite as much the impress of his own as of Schiller's genius; but his work as
a whole represents admirably the spirit of the original.
The following is his translation of the scene in which
Wallenstein entreats Max not to desert him (Act iii. sc.
18 of "Wallenstein's Death"—Act ii. sc. 6 in the translation):—

> "*Wal.*   Max, remain with me.
> Go you not from me, Max ! Hark ! I will tell thee—
> How when at Prague, our winter-quarters, thou
> Wert brought into my tent a tender boy,
> Not yet accustomed to the German winters ;

Thy hand was frozen to the heavy colours ;
Thou wouldst not let them go.
At that time did I take thee in my arms,
And with my mantle did I cover thee ;
I was thy nurse, no woman could have been
A kinder to thee ; I was not ashamed
To do for thee all little offices,
However strange to me ; I tended thee
Till life returned ; and when thine eyes first opened,
I had thee in my arms. Since then, when have I
Altered my feelings t'wards thee ? Many thousands
Have I made rich, presented them with lands ;
Rewarded them with dignities and honours ;
Thee have I loved : my heart, myself, I gave
To thee ! They all were aliens : thou wert
Our child and inmate. Max ! thou canst not leave me :
It cannot be ; I may not, will not think
That Max can leave me.
    Max.   O my God !
    Wal.   I have
Held and sustained thee from thy tottering childhood.
What holy bond is there of natural love,
What human tie, that does not knit thee to me ?
I love thee, Max ! What did thy father for thee,
Which I too have not done, to the height of duty ?
Go hence, forsake me, serve thy Emperor ;
He will reward thee with a pretty chain
Of gold ; with his ram's fleece will he reward thee ;
For that the friend, the father of thy youth,
For that the holiest feeling of humanity,
Was nothing worth to thee.
    Max.   O God ! how can I
Do otherwise ? Am I not forced to do it ?
My oath—my duty—honour——
    Wal.   How ? thy duty ?
Duty to whom ? Who art thou ? Max ! bethink thee
What duties mayst thou have ? If I am acting
A criminal part toward the Emperor.

It is my crime, not thine.   Dost thou belong
To thine own self ?   Art thou thine own commander?
Stand'st thou, like me, a freeman in the world,
That in thy actions thou shouldst plead free agency?
On me thou'rt planted, I am thy Emperor;
To obey me, to belong to me, this is
Thy honour, this a law of nature to thee!
And if the planet, on the which thou liv'st
And hast thy dwelling, from its orbit starts,
It is not in thy choice, whether or no
Thou'lt follow it;—unfelt, it whirls thee onward
Together with his ring and all his moons.
With little guilt stepp'st thou into this contest;
Thee will the world not censure, it will praise thee,
For that thou heldst thy friend more worth to thee
Than names and influences more removed."

Immediately before his death (Act v. sc. 3 of the same
play—in the translation, Act v. sc. 1), Wallenstein, in
conversation with the Countess Tertzky, mourns the loss
of Max :—

"*Wal.* I shall grieve down this blow, of that I'm conscious:
What does not man grieve down ?   From the highest,
As from the vilest thing of every day,
He learns to wean himself: for the strong hours
Conquer him.   Yet I feel what I have lost
In him.   The bloom is vanished from my life.
For oh, he stood beside me, like my youth !
Transformed for me the real to a dream,
Clothing the palpable and familiar
With golden exhalations of the dawn.
Whatever fortunes wait my future toils,
The beautiful is vanished—and returns not."

Earlier in this scene there are some splendid lines, in
which Wallenstein, looking out into the night, describes
what he sees.   This is Coleridge's rendering of them :—

    " *Wal.* There is a busy motion in the Heaven,
    The wind doth chase the flag upon the tower,
    Fast sweep the clouds, the sickle of the moon,
    Struggling, darts snatches of uncertain light.
    No form of star is visible ! That one
    White stain of light, that single glimmering yonder,
    Is from Cassiopeia, and therein
    Is Jupiter. (*A pause.*) But now
    The blackness of the troubled element hides him ! "

To these extracts may be added the song sung by
Thecla when her mind is oppressed by a presentiment
of coming evil. The English verses are by Charles
Lamb, and Coleridge praises them for " having caught
the happiest manner of our old ballads : "—

    " The clouds are blackening, the storms threatening,
      The cavern doth mutter, the greenwood moan ;
    Billows are breaking, the damsel's heart aching,
      Thus in the dark night she singeth alone,
        Her eye upward roving :
    The world is empty, the heart is dead surely,
      In this world plainly all seemeth amiss ;
    To thy heaven, Holy One, take home thy little one,
      I have partaken of all earth's bliss,
        Both living and loving."

CHAPTER XII.

IN WEIMAR.

DURING the five years of life which remained to Schiller his work was frequently interrupted by illness. One of his lungs gradually wasted away, and he was seldom altogether free from pain. In other respects he considered himself fortunate, for he was no longer burdened by the duties either of a professor or of an editor, and could devote his whole time to congenial labour. Few men of genius have had so happy a domestic life as Schiller. "Heaven had given him in his wife and children," as he once wrote, "nothing but joy." Shortly before their departure from Jena, a third child, a daughter, had been born; and in 1804 the family was completed by the birth of another daughter. Schiller was seen at his best in his relations to his children, whom he treated with a charming mixture of playfulness and tenderness. Often he was found "romping" with them; and he caused much merriment by the inflexible rule that, in order to kiss him, they should climb to his face without help. He was remarkably hospitable, and at his table there was always good talk, free, bright, and open. Their most frequent guest was Lotte's sister,

Caroline, for whom he retained all the affection she had excited in the early days of their intimacy.

The Duke and Duchess of Weimar were proud to have Schiller in their capital, and showed him unfailing kindness; and he sincerely responded to their goodwill. Wieland he seldom saw, but they were not on unfriendly terms. This could not be said of Schiller's relation to Herder, who in his last years (he died in 1803) became reserved and morose, hostile to all the intellectual movements of his age, and bitterly deploring that his own achievements had fallen so far below his hopes. Both from Schiller and Goethe, therefore, he held aloof, although they would willingly have conciliated him. Now that Schiller was permanently in Weimar, his friendship with Goethe was, if possible, still more firmly established. If they were at home, a week seldom passed without their seeing each other; and when either was unwell, they maintained a steady correspondence.

Among his other duties Goethe acted as director of the Weimar theatre, and he was delighted to have the advantage of Schiller's aid. They became virtually joint directors, and never perhaps was a theatre conducted with a higher aim. So high, indeed, was their aim, that the public of Weimar and the surrounding country often failed to comprehend it, and would have been well pleased to see the directorate in less ambitious hands. Goethe and Schiller not only took pains in the selection of pieces for representation : they strove to found a great school of acting. In this task Goethe found his friend of the utmost service; for while his own manner was cold, Schiller invited the players to his house, praised them generously when he was satisfied with their performances, and offered them advice as if he were asking them to do him a favour.

It was suggested by Goethe that in order to provide the theatre with an adequate repertory, they should make a collection of good German plays, and "adapt" a number of foreign masterpieces. Schiller cordially assented, and, while Goethe finished his rendering of Voltaire's "Mahomet," set to work on "Macbeth," of which he produced a version that long kept possession of the German stage. To the end of his career he occupied himself at intervals with labours of this kind; but his highest energies were of course given to original work, and when we consider the state of his health, it is astonishing that he was able to make so many and such solid contributions to enduring literature. He had apparently a dim presentiment of early death, and was animated by a desire to force the brief period which was granted to him to yield the fruits of an ampler opportunity. When he had accomplished one scheme, he was ill at ease until he had devised another; and the results indicated on the whole a steady approach to his own high ideal of excellence.

Many years before, during his solitary residence at Bauerbach, it had occurred to him that he might find a fit theme for tragedy in the fate of Mary Stuart; and by study of Robertson and Hume he made himself familiar with the facts of her history. Having completed "Wallenstein," he returned to this idea, and in settling in Weimar he took with him three acts of his new play. The work was concluded early in the summer of 1800 in Ettersburg, a country-house of the Duke of Weimar; and on the 15th of June the first representation took place on the Weimar stage. It was played, he wrote to Körner, "with all the success he could have wished." "At last," he added, "I begin to be master of the dramatic faculty, and to understand my craft." Among many other suggestions which offered themselves, he decided promptly for "The Maid of Orleans" as his next subject. To Goethe he complained that his material would not easily "arrange itself in a few great masses;" but he overcame this difficulty, and before the end of 1800 he had finished more than half of the tragedy. In April 1801 the whole work was given to Goethe, who in returning it spoke of it as "so thorough, so good, so beautiful, that he knew nothing with which to compare it." Circumstances prevented "The Maid of Orleans" from being at once produced in Weimar; but in many other German theatres it was received with greater enthusiasm than had been stirred by any of Schiller's previous works. This was due not only to its art, but to the appropriateness of the Maid's patriotic devotion at a time when the independence of Germany was threatened by the rapidly advancing power of France.

After the completion of "The Maid of Orleans," there was a slight pause in Schiller's activity, as he could not bring himself to make a final choice between several dramatic plans. In autumn (1801) he took advantage of this interval to go with Lotte and Caroline to Dresden, where the Körners welcomed them with all the old affection. Part of the time was happily spent in the summer-house in Loschwitz, in which, sixteen years before, Schiller had found so peaceful a contrast to the storm and misery of his life in Mannheim. When in Dresden before, he

had paid little attention to its treasures of art; but
Goethe had helped him to a higher stage, and now he
visited with delight both public collections and private
studios, and carried away many vivid impressions, especially of ancient marbles. They returned by Leipsic, and
here Schiller had an opportunity of seeing to how great
a height he had risen in the esteem of his countrymen.
In honour of his visit "The Maid of Orleans" was represented, and at the end of the first act shouts of "Live
Friedrich Schiller!" broke from all parts of the theatre.
At the close the spectators hastened out, and waited
for him. When he appeared every head was uncovered,
and he was received in respectful silence. A lane was
formed, along which he and his friends passed; and here
and there, it is said, fathers raised their children to their
shoulders, whispering, "That is he! that is he!"

In 1802, Schiller was deeply grieved by tidings of his
mother's death. His sister Louise was now the wife of
a village pastor, and on hearing of the illness of their
mother, who had been living for some time in Stuttgart,
took her to the parsonage, where she was tenderly cared
for. Schiller begged that she might put herself in the
hands of his old friend Von Hoven, in Ludwigsburg,
and sent money to provide for all expenses; but she was
too ill to be moved. She was proud of her famous son,
and two days before her death asked for a medallion
portrait of him, and pressed it to her heart. "God will
reward you," she wrote, "for all your kindness to me.
Ah, there is not in the world such another son!"

The letter announcing her death was received on the
day (the 29th of April 1802) on which Schiller took possession of the house in Weimar that is now a place of

pilgrimage to multitudes of hero-worshippers. It was a small but convenient dwelling, pleasantly situated, with a garden behind. It had been occupied by the British Consul-General, Mr Mellish, an intimate friend both of Schiller and Goethe; and from him Schiller bought it, obtaining part of the money by the sale of his garden-house near Jena. The rooms on the top floor, with a southern aspect, were set apart for Schiller's use; and here, in his quiet "study," he spent the day at work. His table stood at the window, which, in accordance with his wish, was draped with a curtain of crimson silk, as the reddish glimmer on the paper stimulated his fancy.

In this year (1802) Schiller had the satisfaction, such as it was, of being raised to noble rank. Although so much liked by the Duke and Duchess, he had not hitherto been "Hoffähig,"—that is, he had not possessed the right of appearing at Court. His wife possessed the right by birth, but had lost it by her marriage with a commoner. This state of things caused some inconvenience; and the Duke, anxious to give Schiller a decided proof of his respect, resolved to have the difficulty removed. Application was therefore made to the Imperial Court for his elevation to the "nobility" of the Holy Roman Empire, on the ground that he had done high service by his historical writings, and by the influence he had exerted through his poetry on "the spirit of the German language." The claim was considered good; and on the 16th of November his patent was handed to him by the Duke. "You must have laughed," Schiller wrote to Wilhelm von Humboldt, "when you heard of our rise in rank. It was an idea of our Duke; and since it has happened I can take some pleasure in it, for Lolo's [Lotte's] and the children's sake." "Lolo" wrote to a friend that Schiller was "quite innocent in the matter," and that that pleased her, as "she would have considered it beneath his character to seek for an honour."

During the last months of 1801 and the early months of 1802, he occupied himself in producing a version of Gozzi's "Turandot." After some hesitation he then began "The Bride of Messina," on the plan of which he had been meditating for many months. For some time he felt that he was not in the right mood for a drama in which he was to make so close an approach to the Hellenic spirit; but he at last attuned his mind to his work by reading several tragedies of Æschylus in Stolberg's translation. "Not for years," he wrote to Körner, after finishing them, "have I been penetrated with so much respect as by these highly poetic works." "The Bride of Messina" appeared on the 19th of March 1803; and, according to Schiller's report to Körner, the impression it made was "unusually strong." "For myself," he wrote, "I may venture to say, that in this representation I received for the first time the impression of a true tragedy." A month afterwards "The Maid of Orleans" was produced for the first time in Weimar, and Körner was informed that "the piece had gone charmingly."

In the interval between the appearance of these two plays, Schiller was delighted by the representation of "The Natural Daughter"—a play at which Goethe had worked in silence, wishing to surprise his friend with it. Had they not known each other, it would never have been written: Goethe had ceased to do anything for the stage, and his old desire for this kind of distinction was revived by Schiller's enthusiasm. Schiller himself, after finishing " The Bride of Messina," could not at once undertake another great work, but gave a German form to two comedies by Picard—"Encore des Ménechmes," and "Médiocre et Rampant; ou le moyen de Parvenir." The latter he called "The Parasite;" the former, "The Nephew as Uncle."

In the autumn of 1803 Schiller was presented in the Weimar Palace to the King of Sweden, who begged him to accept a diamond ring as an expression of gratitude for the manner in which he had spoken of the Swedes in his history of the Thirty Years' War. His historical writings were now, however, far from his thoughts; imaginative work alone deeply interested him. And at this time he was engaged on a drama in which he was striving to attain to heights loftier than any to which he had hitherto risen—"William Tell." When Goethe visited Switzerland in 1797, he was so impressed by the scenes associated with William Tell that he resolved to make the legend the subject of an epic poem. The whole scheme rapidly took shape, and on his return he talked of it frequently to Schiller. "In Schiller's mind," he said to Eckermann, "my landscapes and acting figures formed themselves to a drama; and as I had other things to do, I resigned my subject to him, whereupon he wrote his admirable poem." In reality Schiller does not seem to have thought of making Tell the hero of a tragedy before 1802; and Goethe's memory may have been misled by the fact that Schiller had then many questions to ask him about the scenes which were to form the background of the play. When, late in 1803, he had fairly entered on his work, he was oppressed by its difficulties: he had, however, a strong persuasion that he was contending with matter which it would be thoroughly worth while to conquer. "If the gods permit me," he wrote to Körner, "to express what is in my brain, it will be a powerful thing, and will shake the boards of Germany."

Unfortunately, towards the close of the year, when he was thoroughly in the spirit of his work, his attention was distracted by the famous visit of Madame de Staël to Weimar. Never had any one produced in the little capital so strong a "sensation." By her restless vivacity, her endless inquiries, her rapid criticisms, she amazed and disturbed a society which was more accessible to serious thought than to lively controversy, to humour than to wit. Schiller had too much respect for genius in all its forms not to be attracted by so brilliant an intellect; and he sacrificed many hours to have the pleasure of talking with her. Yet in the end he could probably hardly have told whether he liked or disliked her. To Körner he wrote that she was "the most educated and the cleverest woman" he had ever known, and that she "really interested him." He added, however: "She takes away all poetry from me, and I almost wonder that I am still capable of doing anything." She remained more than two months; and when she had gone, Schiller wrote, "I feel very much as if I had recovered from a severe illness." But his "severe illness" had not prevented him from finishing "William Tell;" and on the 17th of March 1804 it was acted, Goethe having exerted himself to the utmost extent of his power to secure that the players should do it justice. Körner was, as usual, informed of the result. "'Tell' is more effective on the stage," Schiller wrote, "than any of my other pieces, and the performance gave me great pleasure. I feel that I am gradually mastering the secret of dramatic art."

Soon after the completion of "William Tell," Schiller received an intimation that if he chose he might be asked to settle in Berlin. Strong as were the attractions which bound him to Weimar, he could not but feel that this change would be advantageous. In Berlin he would be connected with a great theatre, and he would be able not only to improve his circumstances, but to make provision for his family. Accordingly he started almost immediately with Lotte and their children, arriving on the 1st of May 1804. They remained upwards of a fortnight, and Schiller was everywhere received with the highest honour. The leading men of letters waited upon him, and at the theatre several of his plays were produced with more than ordinary care. He had an interview with Queen Louise, during which his eldest son Karl and the Crown Prince, as Schiller wrote to Körner, became good friends. The matter about which he had come, however, was not talked of until the day before his departure, when the Cabinet Councillor, Von Beyme, with whom he dined at Potsdam, told him that the King would be pleased to have him in Berlin, and was willing to accede to any terms that Schiller himself cared to propose. On his return he consulted Goethe, and, after much consideration, wrote to Von Beyme that, although he could not permanently leave Weimar, he would gladly spend some months every year in Berlin, and that this plan would make it necessary for him to have a pension of 2000 thalers. The letter was never answered; but Schiller had no reason to regret the incident, for the Duke of

Weimar, alarmed at the prospect of losing him, readily agreed to double his salary.

Before going to Berlin, Schiller had decided that the history of the false Demetrius should form the subject of his next drama. In summer, however, during a visit to Jena (when his youngest daughter was born), he caught so severe a cold that " Demetrius " and all other work had to be laid aside for a time. At the beginning of winter another cold prostrated him, and feeling too ill to undertake original writing, he began a translation of " Phèdre," which he successfully accomplished in about four weeks.

During this last period of Schiller's life his mind was so absorbed by the drama that other forms of poetry occupied him only at rare intervals. In these intervals, however, he produced a considerable number of poems that are in every way worthy of his genius. To the best of his ballads he made two additions—" Hero and Leander " (1801), and " The Count of Hapsburg " (1803). In the first of these pieces he scarcely succeeds in rendering the charm of youthful passion, but he rises to true greatness of tone in depicting the ruthless play of natural forces with human happiness. The second ballad presents a scene in which Rudolph of Hapsburg yields his favourite horse to a priest who is hurrying with the sacrament to a dying man. The horse thus honoured is afterwards considered too sacred to be used for less noble objects, and the priest foretells that the pious Count will be brilliantly rewarded. At the coronation of Rudolph in Aix-la-Chapelle this incident is celebrated by a poet whom the new monarch recognises as the priest that had prophesied his future greatness. The poem has all the energy and colour of Schiller's early ballads, and is marked by a fine appreciation of the romance and the mysticism of the medieval spirit.

Of Schiller's other poems belonging to this period, the most elaborate is "The Homage of the Arts" ("Die Huldigung der Künste"), a "lyrical play" presented at the Weimar theatre in 1804, in honour of the Russian Princess who had just been married to the heir of the Duke of Weimar. It is an allegory in which the genius of beauty appears, surrounded by figures representing the various arts. The genius of beauty indicates the source of all art in the human mind; and then the arts, each in a few brilliant lines, celebrate the part which they severally play in adorning and dignifying ordinary life. Schiller here expresses in noble forms his sense of the lofty destinies of art, and his conviction that in order to fulfil these destinies it must not limit itself to reality, but range freely and joyfully in an ideal world. In lines addressed to Goethe (1801) on the completion of his translation of "Mahomet" ("An Goethe"), Schiller had touched on other aspects of art, generously recognising the debt which the world owes to the high thought and stately march of the French classic drama. The effect of this poem was balanced by another, "The German Muse" ("Die Deutsche Muse"), also written in 1801, rejoicing in the freedom with which German poetry had been able to develop itself through its independence of the patronage of great Courts.

A more imaginative poem than any of these, although not purer in form, is "Cassandra" (1802), in which Schiller gives a new and deeper meaning to the legend that Cassandra was doomed to misery in consequence

of the neglect of her warnings. He develops with
remarkable power the conception that misery is the
inevitable accompaniment of a deep observation of the
world, if not associated with the perception of an ideal
life in which alone man is free and happy. This
was the prevailing thought of the lyrics which sprang
from the first rush of feeling after his abandonment of
philosophy and history for poetry; and it is the prevailing thought of nearly all the most striking lyrics produced in his latest period. It recurs in his lines " At
the Beginning of the new Century " ("Am Antritt des
neuen Jahrhunderts "), " Longing " (" Sehnsucht "), and
in "The Pilgrim " ("Der Pilgrim ")—the latter written
in 1803, the two former in 1801. In these and other
lyrics he shows a profound consciousness of the limi-
tations, the contradictions, the vain struggles of daily
existence; but high above all gleams the ideal realm
untouched by earthly imperfection. The contrast is
drawn in lines as firm as those of former years, but with
calmer feeling and a more delicate touch.

CHAPTER XIII.

SCHILLER'S LAST DRAMAS.

THE dramatic genius of Schiller manifests itself with such splendid power in "Wallenstein," that we naturally take up his next work, "Mary Stuart," with high expectations. Of all his later dramas, however, this is the one in which we find fewest traces of his free creative energy. In the treatment of the closing scenes of Mary's career, it would be possible to depict her as the most brilliant representative of the forces which fought so hard in the sixteenth century for Catholic and mediæval institutions against the advancing tide of modern ideas. Schiller appears to have deliberately neglected this element of interest, but he does not compensate us by fine conceptions of individual character. Whatever side we may take in the controversies regarding Mary, her name inevitably suggests to modern readers the Queen Mary of 'The Abbot'—the fascinating woman who conquers all hearts, and who is never more romantic than when, with generous confidence in her rival, she steps on board the vessel that is to bear her to her fate. In Schiller's play she has no characteristics of mind or heart that appeal strongly to the imagination. We see only a natural longing for liberty; her actions, her feelings, her thoughts, are without distinction of any kind, and sometimes they indicate astonishing poverty of resource. In the scene, for instance, at the end of the third act, one listens with amazement to her violent tirade against Elizabeth. It was a bold stroke to depart so far from history as to bring the two queens together; but it might have been justified had the opportunity been brilliantly made use of. But we expect from Queen Mary something better than the wild rage of a virago. Had she been such a character as confronts us in this interview, Queen Elizabeth would have had little reason for imprisoning her, and none at all for putting her to death. Queen Elizabeth is not more happily presented. She is animated throughout by spite and jealousy; and the death of the Queen of Scots is therefore deprived of every element of grandeur with which it was in reality associated. It is hardly going too far to say that the two queens produce a less poetic impression in the poet's interpretation of their struggle than in the bare facts of their history.

There is more of Schiller's dramatic power in his presentation of the gloomy Burleigh and the statesmanlike Shrewsbury. Many fine traits are also discernible in the wavering resolves of Leicester; but his character, on the whole, is too shadowy—the conduct attributed to him is sometimes too arbitrary—to sustain the interest which he arouses in the early part of the play. In Mortimer, Schiller attempted to introduce a truly tragic figure; but his love for Mary has the appearance of being forced upon him by the poet, and his death is slightly melodramatic.

These defects are much more visible when the play is represented in a foreign language than when it is given in the original, for in the latter its faults are for the moment concealed by the splendour of its diction. When Schiller wrote " Mary Stuart," he had perfectly mastered the " mighty line" by which, like Marlowe among English dramatists, he is distinguished among the dramatists of Germany. The effect is magnificent when his rhetoric is associated with lofty thought and feeling ; and while we are under its influence, it seems almost to communicate some of its own swelling pomp to thought and feeling which are by no means lofty. Another characteristic of this play is the almost perfect technical skill with which its materials are combined. In no other play by Schiller does the tale unfold itself with a movement so regular and so steadily progressive. The scenes in each act, while varied enough to keep curiosity awake, are grouped around a central point of interest, and one act is fitted accurately into another so as to produce a symmetrical whole. In the first act the elements of the tragic conflict are all, either directly or indirectly, indicated ; in the second, we see the struggle in progress ; in the third, it is driven rapidly to the crisis ; in the fourth, in strict accordance with Aristotelian rule, there is the change of circumstance which prepares for the end ; in the last, the catastrophe. A deeper source of interest, however, is an occasional outburst of true poetic feeling, as in the pathetic scene where Mary, liberated for a moment, runs forward from among the trees, and rejoices like a child in her freedom.

In this scene she is accompanied by her maid, Hannah Kennedy, who, when Mary utters passionate exclamations of delight, reminds her that she is not really free, and that she does not see the walls of her prison simply because they are concealed by trees.   Mary interrupts her : [1]—

> " Thanks, kind thanks, to you, ye trees,
>   That hide my prison walls so well !
>   I dream of liberty and joy—
>   Oh why so sweet a dream dispel ?
>   Above me spreads the azure sky,
>   And there, unfettered, roves the eye
>   Through endless spaces happily.
>   Far off, where grey hills pierce the mist,
>   Towards my kingdom's bounds I glance ;
>   And yonder clouds, that southward drive,
>   They seek the distant sea of France.
>   Ye ships of air that freely roam,
>   Oh greet for me my youth's dear home :
>   Beneath the yoke I sadly bend,
>   I cannot other herald send !
>   Your path hath ever open been,—
>   Not ruled are ye by this stern queen ! "

Kennedy still expostulates, but Mary again turns aside her warnings, pointing to a fisherman who trims his boat, and trying to persuade herself that he may perhaps bear her to her friends.   The scene ends with a cry of joy when the bugle-note of a passing hunting-party reminds Mary of the days when on Scottish heaths she too joined the chase.

In "The Maid of Orleans" ("Die Jungfrau von Orleans") Schiller found a subject far more congenial to his powers than in "Mary Stuart."   His imagination was baffled by intricate subtleties of feeling ; it worked

---

[1] The translations in this chapter are by the author of the present volume.

freely only when the effects at which it aimed were grand and massive. The sublime simplicity of the Maid of Orleans was therefore well adapted to his genius, and his conception of her character is surpassed by none of his creations in dramatic truth and force. Many characters pass over the stage, and the stir of battle is as frequent as in any of Shakespeare's historical dramas : but we never lose sight of the central figure ; every incident has some relation to her heroic destinies. The dramatic prologue places us in the midst of the rustic scenes where she has passed her youth, and where she receives the helmet which is to her the sign that the time has come for the deliverance of her people. Around her stand her father, Raimund (her lover), and Bertrand, by whose means the miraculous helmet has come to her hands ; and they talk of the French being forced to yield. For a time she listens silently, but at last her enthusiasm finds expression ; and in these her first utterances the key-note of the play is struck.

"*Joan.* Surrender ! Treaties ! Speak not of them more !
Equipped for fight, the sure deliverer comes !
At Orleans the fortune of the foe
Shall be destroyed : for judgment he is ripe.
The Maid draws nigh, her sickle in her hand,
To mow the lordly harvest of his pride ;
And she with scorn shall pluck from heaven's heights
The fame which he has hung upon the stars.
Despair not ! Fly not ! Ere the fields are touched
To gold, ere yonder crescent moon is full,
The English steeds shall elsewhere slake their thirst
Than in the waters of the bright Loire.
    Bertrand. Alas ! no more are miracles performed.
    Joan. Still shines the day of miracles ! A dove,
Snow-white, with eagle's force, shall bold attack

These vultures, birds of doom that rend our land.
Proud Burgundy, a traitor to the State,
She shall with might strike down ; and Talbot, too.
The hundred-handed Titan, storming heaven,
And Salisbury, blasphemer of the Church,
And with them all these shameful islanders,
Like flocks of lambs, she shall before her drive.
The Lord will be her aid, the God of battles ;
His trembling creature He will choose, and show
His power and glory by a tender maid.

    Thibaut. What spirit agitates the lass ?
    Raimund.   It is
The helmet makes her speak in warlike tones.
Behold your daughter ! See, her eye is flashing,
And glowing fire doth sparkle from her cheeks.

    Joan. Who says this realm shall fall ? This land of fame,
The loveliest land on which the sun doth shine,
The paradise of lands, beloved of God,
As if it were the apple of His eye—
Shall *it* endure the chains of foreign lords ?
Here broke the pagans' might ; here first was raised
The wonder-working Cross ; and in this soil
St Louis' sacred dust in calmness rests ;
From here the Holy City was o'ercome.

    Bertrand. What means her speech ? And whence has she
        received
This revelation ? God has given you,
Thibaut, a marvellous child.

    Joan.   Henceforth, 'tis said,
Our native kings shall not rule over us ;
The king, who never dies, must disappear—
The king, who guards the sacred plough, protects
The common land, and fruitful makes the earth,
Who leads downtrodden serfs to liberty,
Who gladly ranges cities round his throne,
Assists the weak, and terrifies the base,
Who envy knows not, since he is the chief,
Who is a man, yet feels an angel's pity.

The throne of kings in golden splendour shines,
The refuge of the lost ; beside it Power
And Mercy stand ; the guilty dread its might,
The just in confidence approach, and safe
Do with the lions play that guard its base.
The foreign king, whose father's bones repose
In other lands, can he our country love ?
And can her sons in him a father find,
Whose heart responds not to her kindly speech,
Who grew not with her youths to manhood's strength ? "

In the first act we see Charles VII., his councillors and
courtiers ; and a few well-selected circumstances reveal
the utter exhaustion of their resources, and the depth
of their despair. Suddenly the Maid appears, not, as
in history, after much painful effort, but as one before
whom the enemy has already begun to fly in wild terror.
By the grandeur of her character, and by manifest tokens
of divine favour, she instantly obtains the confidence of
the chiefs of the nation, and infuses into them some of
her own indomitable courage. Between the first and
second acts the English are supposed to be driven from
Orleans ; then during the whole of the second and the
greater part of the third act, the war continues, the
Maid leading the French armies from victory to victory.
At the close of the third act she overtakes Lionel, one
of the English commanders ; and suddenly her inward
life undergoes a complete transformation. She cannot
slay him as she has slain all other Englishmen who have
fallen into her power, for he fills her heart with an ab-
sorbing love. It must be admitted that this sudden
change is a little perplexing. Hitherto she has been an
epic rather than a dramatic figure, sublime in the consciousness of her mission, with superhuman energy, but

calm and self-controlled. It seems scarcely in keeping
with her character, apparently so remote from earthly
passions, to descend by a bound from her serene heights
to the humbler level of ordinary women, especially as
we have not been permittted to see anything in Lionel
that would make her love intelligible. If, however, we
concede to Schiller the right to attribute this experience
to his heroine, it is impossible not to admire the art
with which he traces its effects on her nature. All
at once she becomes shy, self-conscious, a creature of
passing fears and hopes; we find it difficult to realise
that she can ever have been the guiding genius of a
mighty nation. When Agnes Sorrel, whom the king
loves, comes to confide in her, assuming that she belongs
to another sphere, the Maid shows for the first time, by
many little touches, that she too has need of sympathy.
Accused by her father of witchcraft, she hangs down her
head before the assembled court, unable to give the true
meaning of a career from which in her heart she has
turned aside. And so, accompanied by the faithful
rustic who loved her in the days of her obscurity, she
flies, and wanders in misery through the land, until she
is taken prisoner by the English. In the English camp
she endures bitter indignity; but, gradually surrounded
by the enemy, she recovers her self-possession; and at
last, when she sees the French defeated and King Charles
in danger, her heroism shines forth anew in all its star-
like radiance. The next scenes are so full of vitality
and poetry that only a pedant would object to Schiller's
free handling of history. With the strength of a goddess, she snaps her bonds asunder, snatches a sword
from a soldier, and hurries to the field, where she saves

the king, turns the tide of victory, and dies in peace, enjoying the restored confidence and reverence of her countrymen.

This is a thoroughly poetical creation, grandly formed, and breathing the breath of life. The other characters, although necessarily very subordinate, are not less true to nature. To name only a few, there is genuine vitality in the weak but kindly king, in the valiant Dunois, in the wayward Burgundy, whom, in a scene full of grace and vivacity, the Maid reconciles to the friends with whom he has been contending; and a striking contrast is presented in the characters of the tender and generous Agnes Sorrel and the treacherous Isabeau, the king's mother. The Maid's father and sisters, rough, superstitious, but with affection at the bottom of their hearts, are such characters as would be naturally formed in the quiet country with its simple customs and half-heathenish faith. Of the English characters, by far the most impressive is Talbot; and the ideal passions of the Maid find their most effective foil in the mood of bitter cynicism in which he dies.

> " *Talbot.* Madness, the victory is thine ! I yield.
> The gods themselves with dulness fight in vain.
> Exalted Reason, radiant Daughter sprung
> From head divine, wise founder of the world,
> Conductor of the stars—what art thou, then,
> If, to the tail of Folly's mad horse bound,
> With powerless cries, and knowing well thy state,
> Thou must with that drunk beast plunge darkly down
> To the abyss ? Accursèd he who gives
> His life to great and worthy aims, and forms
> His plans with prudent mind; the Fools' King rules
> The world.

Lionel.   My lord, the moments of thy life
Are few. To thy Creator turn thy thoughts.
     Talbot. Had we as brave men yielded to the brave,
We might have consolation found in this—
That Fortune, ever changing, turns her sphere;
But to be crushed by vulgar jugglery!
Deserved our toilsome life no graver end ?
     Lionel. My lord, farewell ! If I survive the fight,
The meed of tears I owe, I'll freely pay ;
But I am summoned to the field by Fate,
Who still uncertain sits and shakes her urn.
In other worlds we meet, but now—farewell !
For friendship long as ours, the parting brief.
     Talbot. It soon is past, and now I do give back
To earth and to the everlasting sun
The atoms which in me have been combined
For pain and joy ; and of the mighty Talbot,
Who filled the world with his renown, is left
A handful of poor dust. So ends our life ;
And all the gain the tedious struggle yields
Is that we heartily despise what once
Appeared to us alluring or sublime,
And learn at last its utter nothingness.

"The Bride of Messina" (" Die Braut von Messina ")
takes us into a wholly different world.   Here Schiller
abandons the methods of the modern drama, and reproduces antique forms.   In close imitation of the Greek
dramatists, he selects an action capable of intense com-
pression, for the development of which few characters
are necessary, while the chorus breaks in from time to
time with its warnings and reflections.   Again following
the example of his models, he assumes that before the
opening scenes much has happened that would in a
modern play gradually lead the characters into the centre of the tragic conflict.   In this instance Schiller did

F.C.—XV.   N not choose a historical subject, because it seemed to him that it would be easier to force an invented action within the necessary limits. The first character who appears is Donna Isabella, the Princess of Messina. In a large pillared hall she addresses the elders of the city, telling them of her two sons, Don Manuel and Don Cæsar, who have cherished towards each other from childhood a bitter hatred, and who, since their father's recent death, have carried on war. They unite, however, in love for their mother; and through her intercession they have agreed to lay down their arms, and are immediately to return to the palace. Soon they confront each other, and after some explanations they are frankly reconciled. While they converse, a messenger arrives and whispers to Don Cæsar that the beautiful woman for whom he has been searching is in Messina; and he hurries away. The beautiful woman is Beatrice, whom Don Cæsar had accidentally seen at his father's funeral in a remote convent. Don Manuel then narrates to the Chorus an adventure which had brought him to a lovely lady whose heart he has won :—

> " Five months have fled, and still my father's power
> Did rule the land ; beneath his yoke he bent
> With tyrannous sway the neck of fiery youth.
> I knew no joy but in the clash of arms,
> And in the warlike rapture of the chase.
> At eve, when we had hunted all the day
> Along the wooded heights, I left your train,
> And followed close, alone, a snow-white hind.
> Through windings of the vale, through rocky clefts,
> Thickets, and trackless ground o'ergrown with brier,
> The shy and timid beast before me fled :
> I saw it ever near, but sought in vain

A spot that offered chance of happy aim,
Until at length it vanished from my view
Behind a garden-door.   Dismounting swift,
With eager steps I ran, my javelin poised ;
And lo ! the frightened creature trembling lay
Before a nun, who stooped to soothe its fears,
And gently fondled it with tender hands.
I gazed astonished at a scene so strange,
My hunting spear stretched forth in act to strike.
She turned, and in her lustrous eyes I read
A plea for mercy.   Silently we stood,
How long I know not, time we both forgot :
Her glance pierced through my soul, and suddenly
An all-absorbing love transformed my heart.
What then I said, and what the lovely maid
Replied, let no man ask ; it floats before
My vision like a dream of childhood's dawn.
When memory returned, her throbbing heart
Beat fast with passionate glow against my own.
With sudden clang a bell the stillness broke—
A call to vespers ; and as spirits dart
Through air, she quickly vanished from my sight.
    Chorus. Forebodings sad, O Prince, thy words arouse,
For thou hast robbed the awful Powers above ;
Heaven's bride thou hast approached with sinful love ;
Most sacred are the holy cloister's vows.
    Don Manuel. I had but one dear path henceforth to tread,
My wayward, restless longings were subdued ;
From life I had its precious secret plucked.
And as the pilgrim seeks the distant East,
Where on his face the Sun of Promise shines,
So turned my heart with longing and with hope
Towards the spot where brightly glowed its star.
Each day that dawned and sank behind the wave,
Two happy lovers met : in secret wove
Our hearts the bonds that bound them each to each.
The all-beholding eye of Heaven alone
Was trusted witness of our hidden joy ;

We neither sought nor needed other aid.
Oh, these were golden hours, most happy days!
The awful Powers above I had not robbed,
For she who had become for ever mine
Had not enthralled her heart and will with vows."

Don Manuel having explained that an old man sometimes brought messages to her from her unknown
mother, the passage continues :—

" *Don Man.* For months the old man hinted that the day
Which would restore her to her kin drew near ;
But yesterday he plainly bade her hope
For full disclosure of her destiny
With this day's dawn ; my purpose swift I formed,
And swift fulfilled ; by night I sought the maid,
And brought her to Messina secretly.
Chorus. A deed of robbery and violence !
Forgive, O Prince, the word of bold reproof ;
The right to warn belongs to prudent age,
When reckless youth by passion is misled.
Don Man. Beside the convent of the Merciful,
Amid a peaceful garden's tranquil scenes,
Which cannot be by curious eyes o'erlooked,
I parted from her, hastening to this place
To be unto my brother reconciled.
With timid heart she waits, expecting not
That soon with queenly splendour she shall come,
And on a lofty pedestal of fame
Be placed before all proud Messina's gaze.
For not again shall she her lover see
Save in the high magnificence of State,
Surrounded by the chorus of his knights.
I wish not that Don Manuel's beloved
Should as a homeless fugitive appear
Before his mother ; as a royal bride
She shall with royal dignity approach
The palace of my fathers.

Chorus. Prince, we wait
For thy commands.
  Don Man. Reluctantly I left
Her arms, but she shall still my thoughts employ.
Now ye shall go with me to where the Moors
The merchandise of Eastern lands display,—
Their fabrics rare and works of delicate art.
And lovely sandals first select, her feet
To guard and grace; and for her flowing robe
The tissue of the Indies choose, gleaming
As gleams the snow that lies on Etna's top,
Nearest the sun ; and let it lightly float,
Like morning mist, around her youthful limbs.
And purple let her girdle be, with lines
Of gold inwoven, binding witchingly
The tunic underneath her modest breast.
Her mantle, too, of dazzling silk, shall shine
In purple hues ; and ye shall not forget
To furnish bracelets for her graceful arms,
And pearls, and corals, wondrous gifts bestowed
By ocean's goddess. Let a diadem
Of costly gems entwine her waving locks,
The fiery, glowing ruby, emulous,
Contending with the emerald's flashing rays.
Her ample veil, like bright and airy clouds,
Shall circle round her splendid form ;
And the enchanting whole ye shall complete
By myrtle wreathed upon her virgin brows.
  Chorus. All shall be done, O prince, as thou command'st.
  Don Man. Then from my stables lead a palfrey forth,
White as Apollo's steeds, with purple cloth,
Its bridle and its trappings rich adorned
With precious stones, for it shall bear my queen !
And ye yourselves shall ready be, amid
The joyous clang of trumpets, with the pomp
Of knightly state, to guide your princess home."

  Both brothers love the same person ; and ultimately

she proves to be their sister. Before Beatrice's birth Donna Isabella had a dream which was interpreted to mean that a daughter would cause the ruin of their house. Her husband had therefore ordered the child to be killed; but Donna Isabella had secretly sent her to the convent where she had since lived. Finding Don Manuel with her, Don Cæsar, not yet knowing her relation to them, stabs his brother; and over the body the Chorus, represented by its leaders, Cajetan and Berengar, prepares the mother for tidings of the disaster that has befallen her:—

CAJETAN.

" Through the streets of the cities,
    By sorrow attended,
    Marches misfortune ;
    Darkly it lurks near
    The dwellings of men.
    Here is its summons
    Sounded to-day,
    There on the morrow ;
    Never is any portal passed by.
    The dark, unwished-for,
    Dolorous message,
    Sooner or later
    Reaches each threshold—
    Threshold alike of lowly and high.

BERENGAR.

When in autumn the leaves
From the trees fall away,
When the powers of worn age
Slowly fade and decay,
Nature but calmly submits
To its own ancient law,

To its own changeless wont,—
We watch not its course with shuddering awe.
  But horror, too, O man,
Prepare to meet in earthly life !
With a violent hand
Breaketh fell murder the holiest band ;
To its boat of doom
Snatches grim death
Even youth in its earliest bloom.

CAJETAN.

When clouds in masses sweep the sky,
And bellowing thunder peals,
The power of awful destiny
The boldest heart in secret feels.
But crushing bolts may man destroy
From bright and spotless azure deeps :
He, then, alone is wise who keeps
A moderate heart in hours of joy.
Attempt not lasting peace to find
In fortune's transitory dower :
In thy most prosperous, happy hour,
The secret learn—to be resigned."

The play ends with the death of Don Cæsar, who, learn-ing the truth, slays himself in horror.

In this tragedy we feel throughout, even more strongly than in " Wallenstein," the mysterious working of des-tiny. Man appears as a being subject to dark influences which he cannot sway, and which, if he be doomed to disaster, do not swerve from their course until he has been destroyed. So far, the play maintains the true Hellenic conception ; and Schiller is also consistent in the manner in which he depicts his characters. There is no attempt at fine portraiture : Donna Isabella, her sons, and

Beatrice, are broad types rather than individuals. Don
Manuel and Don Cæsar, indeed, can hardly be spoken
of as separate types, since in both there is essentially the
same note. In other respects, however, the play diverges
widely from the antique spirit. The love of the brothers
for Beatrice, its sentiment, its romance, are entirely
modern; and we feel that for the cravings of so deep a
passion the restrained forms of Greek art do not suffice.
Another difficulty is that, while the Greek religion is behind the action, and determines its course, the characters
profess Christianity. This confusion would not of itself
have greatly impaired the antique character of the play,
for the Christian element is only on the surface, and
does not in any way come into conflict with the Hellenic
doctrine. It is a more serious objection that Schiller
does not exactly reproduce the Greek Chorus, which
stood apart from the action, commenting on it with
perfect impartiality. The Chorus in "The Bride of
Messina" consists of the followers of the two brothers;
and the followers of each represent in some degree the
conflicting aims of their chief. The cause of this
error was probably, as Wilhelm von Humboldt suggested, the modern demand that everything in art shall
have a motive. Schiller could not bring himself to introduce the Chorus simply for its own sake: it was
necessary, he thought, that there should be a reason in
the scheme of his play for its appearance. To the Greeks
the Chorus in a play was a matter of course; it was "like
the sky in a landscape."

It cannot, then, be said that "The Bride of Messina"
is a play either in the genuinely antique or in the genuinely modern spirit. Both elements are combined; and

their union is only mechanical. Nevertheless, the work is one of enduring interest, for its style is almost uniformly grand and melodious. The rhetorical force of many passages, especially of those uttered by the Chorus, could not probably be matched by anything either in the rest of Schiller's writings or in German literature.

In "William Tell" Schiller returned to the path from which he had diverged in "The Bride of Messina;" and as it was the last, so it is in some respects the best, of his complete writings. Some scenes in "Wallenstein" have greater dramatic energy than any in "William Tell," but the latter, as a whole, is more artistically conceived. Here, as in "The Maid of Orleans," Schiller represents passions and struggles which engaged his strongest sympathies; but, even more successfully than in that play, he compels himself to stand aside and to allow his figures to develop in accordance with their own deepest tendencies. The sublime background of the action presented a formidable difficulty, for Schiller had never been in Switzerland, nor had he enjoyed an opportunity elsewhere of studying mountain scenery. Working, however, from his knowledge of the Swabian hills, and combining with this the impressions derived from books, and especially from Goethe's descriptions, he was able not only to see the Alps in fancy, but to catch the spirit of the scenes in which his characters were to unfold themselves. Everywhere we feel the presence of the mountains; we are taken to their high, peaceful valleys, and see the light flash from the distant glaciers; the narrow gorge, the deep abyss, the rushing torrent, the dark pines—all are remembered, and the imagination is stimulated to combine them in a picture at which the poet only hints. The familiar sounds are heard,—the far-off "jodel," the bells "of the high-pasturing kine;" and the Lake of Lucerne we see in storm and in calm, and are made to appreciate the charm of its quiet shores. Although in one brief passage the action is represented as taking place in early winter, the weather throughout is that of summer, and the scenery stands forth in many different aspects,—in bright moonlight, in the splendour of dawn, in the freshness of the morning, in the full glow of day. These varied elements, prominent as they are, are not forced on the attention; they are depicted, not for their own sake, but because without them the course of events would be unintelligible.

The mountaineers, as Schiller describes them, accord perfectly with the land in which they dwell. Here no contrast is suggested between the world within and the world without; there is no trace of the fever of Obermann's "wounded spirit," of Manfred's rage and agony. The people are calm, simple, and strong, loving their mountains and passes, their lakes and valleys, but hardly conscious of them as beautiful or grand—hardly, indeed, thinking of them at all, only feeling that no-where else could they be at home or at peace. They cling to ancient rights, beliefs, and customs; and so peaceful is their temper that they would not, probably, resist slight aggression; but Gessler, the imperial bailiff, gives them no alternative. Under his despotic govern-ment, the honour of their wives and daughters is un-safe; they are threatened with the loss of their posses-sions; they do not enjoy the right of unrestricted move-ment. Against such tyranny they cannot but fling themselves ; and we feel from the beginning that, whatever may be the influences behind their harsh ruler, he must sooner or later go down before the determination of a brave and free race.

Tell does not take the lead in the movement ; he is not even one of the band who secretly vow to deliver their country. Schiller's aim was to exhibit the heroism of a whole people, not merely that of an individual ; and this aim would have been defeated had Tell or any one else been made their chief. Tell, however, in an ideal form, represents all the essential qualities of the popular character. His words breathe the spirit of liberty ; and his manly bearing shows that to be "cabined, cribbed, confined," would be to him worse than a thousand deaths. His limbs have the strength and suppleness that properly belong to the daring climber and huntsman ; he is absolutely fearless, and passes unharmed through dangers that could be faced only by one of his firm nerve and inflexible will. Yet he has the tenderness of a woman, and will risk his life to rescue a lamb that has strayed from the flock. The helpless and the suffering never appeal to him for aid in vain ; and his boys find in him a gentle companion as well as a wise counsellor. His modesty is such that no one ever hears except from common fame of his romantic feats ; and he is so conciliatory that even when reproached for not doing reverence to the insulting symbol of authority set up by Gessler, he is ready to express regret and to promise compliance in future. He does not indulge in extravagant declamation ; nor does he at any time determine his conduct in accordance with large and deeply meditated schemes. When he has anything to do, he dislikes to think much of it beforehand, preferring to trust to the promptings of his pure and loyal instincts. Although deeply saddened by the position of his countrymen, he forms no resolution for their deliverance until the full measure of their wrongs is brought home to him by the mocking injustice with which he himself is treated. He then goes straight to the mark, and rids the cantons of their oppressor, but without any pretension of heroic virtue. As he takes his aim, he thinks not only of himself and of his family, but of his people; and when his mission is accomplished, he mounts to his home in peace, untroubled by a single regret or doubt. In order to bring out the contrast between his deed and mere revolutionary violence, Schiller introduces towards the end the murderer of the Emperor Albert, a man overcome by remorse. The scene is unfortunate, for it suggests that, after all, Tell's action presents a problem about which opinions may differ; but the discord lasts only for a moment. As his countrymen surround his cottage, and offer him the tribute of their gratitude and love, his heroism reveals itself in its full splendour. We see in him a type of lofty patriotism, the incarnation of the energy, simplicity, and truth befitting a man who lives in daily communion with Nature in her noblest as well as her loveliest aspects.

Of the other characters, the three heads of the secret confederation, Stauffacher, Walther Fürst, and Arnold von Melchthal, are the most vigorously conceived,—the first representing the steady impulses of mature life, the second the prudent counsels of old age, the third the vehemence of youth which has been wounded through the affections. There is an admirable type of the old class of Swiss nobles in Freiherr von Attinghausen, an aged man conscious of his dignity, yet ruling his house with patriarchal kindness, and making the cause of his neighbours his own. Gessler has few individual traits, but his violence and brutality are sufficiently displayed to enable us to understand the hatred with which even quiet country-folk conspire against him. Hedwig, Tell's wife, anxious, narrow, and querulous, is an effective foil to her husband's boldness and reserve; yet she is so presented that we cannot dislike her, since her very faults spring in some degree from her love. Bertha, the rich heiress, interests us by the patriotic enthusiasm through which she succeeds in striking a generous spark in her selfish, irresolute lover, Rudenz, the nephew of Attinghausen, who has in vain striven to win him for his country's service. Best of all the female characters, however, is Gertrude, Stauffacher's wife, who has something of Tell's heroic quality. It is she who, in an early scene, suggests to Stauffacher the necessity of resisting the tyrant :—

" *Gertrude.* So grave, my friend ? I scarce do know thee
　　now.
For many days I have in silence watched
How sorrow ploughs deep furrows on thy brow.
Upon thy soul a secret burden weighs;
Oh, hide it not! I am thy faithful wife,
And rightfully may claim to share thy grief :
Confide to me what care doth gnaw thy heart.
Thy industry is blessed, and on thee smiles
Prosperity : thy barns are full, and troops
Of cattle, and of horses nourished well,
Have from the mountains safe returned, to pass

In pleasant stalls the coming winter months.
There stands thy house, rich as a noble's seat ;
Of trunk-wood fair it has been lately reared,
And planned by proper rule; and graciously
Its many windows gleam, and on its walls
Are coats of arms designed in varied hues,
And adages which travellers, lingering, read.

  Stauffacher. Well planned and reared the dwelling stands,
    but, ah !
'Twas built, methinks, upon a tottering base.

  Gert. My Werner, say, what mean thy words ?

  Stauff.   Before
This lime-tree late I sat, as now, well pleased
To gaze upon the work we had achieved.
From Küssnacht rode the bailiff with his men,
And paused in wonder opposite the house.
I rose, and with respect approached the lord
Who represents the Emperor in our midst.
' Whose house is this ? ' he mocking cried, for well
He knew; a prudent answer I returned :—
' This house, sir, is my lord the Emperor's,
And yours, and mine in fief ; ' and he replied,
' I rule this province in the Emperor's name,
And do not choose that peasants should have power
To build fair houses when they please, and live
As if they were the masters of the land ;
I will presume to take that power away.'
Defiantly he then rode on ; but I
Remained with anxious heart, and sadly weighed
His threat.

  Gert. Dear lord and husband, wilt thou take
A word of honest counsel from thy wife ?
Oft to my father, noble Iberg, came
The leaders of the people, and while they spoke,
We sisters sat and span, and heard them read
The parchments of the ancient emperors,
And carefully discuss the country's weal.
Many a word I marked, expressing that

Which is the wise man's thought, the good man's wish;
And still I guard it safe within my heart.
The bailiff hates and seeks to injure thee,
Because by thy advice the men of Schwytz
Refuse to bend beneath the Hapsburg's yoke,
And do with stout and loyal hearts maintain,
As did their ancestors in days of old,
That to the Emperor alone they owe
Allegiance. Say, Werner, if I err.
    Stauff. Such is indeed the source of Gessler's hate.
    Gert. He envies thee because thou livest free
And happy on thine own inheritance,
For he has none.   The Emperor himself
Grants thee thy house in fief, and thou display'st
Thy dwelling as a prince displays his lands:
No power on earth can claim thy reverence
Except the highest power in Christendom.
But haughty Gessler is a younger son,
And save his knightly mantle nought can show:
With jealous eyes he therefore contemplates
The better fortune of each honest man.
Thy ruin long ago he swore ; unscathed
Thou still dost stand ; but wilt thou tamely wait
Till he matures his plans, and safe can strike ?
The prudent man prepares.
    Stauff.   What can be done ?
    Gert. My counsel hear : thou knowest how in Schwytz
All men detest the bailiff's greed and rage.
The men of Uri and of Unterwald,
Be sure, are not less weary of the yoke,
For Landenberg, like Gessler here, misrules
The people of the lands above the lake—
Intelligence of horrid outrage comes
With every boat that touches at our shores.
It were, then, well that some of you, whose thought
Is firm and true, did secretly confer,
And plan to shake this dire oppression off :
High Heaven would not forsake you in your need,—

It would show favour to your righteous cause.
In Uri hast thou ne'er a friend to whom
In confidence thou mightst thy heart reveal?
 Stauff. I know in Uri many valiant men,
And men of station, held in good esteem,
Whose loyal friendship I may freely trust.
Oh, what a storm of dangerous thoughts, my wife,
Dost thou awaken in my quiet breast!
To my unwilling gaze thou dost unfold
My inmost mind in open light of day;
What I in secret ventured not to think,
Thou boldly dost with ready speech express.
But hast thou well considered thy advice?
The clang of arms, the rage of bitter strife,
Into this peaceful vale thou summonest.
Shall we, a feeble band of shepherds, dare
To war against the sovereign of the world?
They wait but for a show of right to send
Their hordes abroad on our unhappy land,
To rule us with a savage conqueror's power,
And with pretence of righteous punishment
To tear the charters of our liberty.
 Gert. Ye, too, are men, with strength to grasp and wield
The battle-axe; and God doth help the brave.
 Stauff. O wife, a horror wild and mad is war;
The shepherd and his flocks alike it smites.
 Gert. Misfortunes Heaven sends must be endured;
A noble heart will ne'er submit to wrong.
 Stauff. Thou hast with pleasure seen our dwelling rise;
The monster, War, would burn it to the ground.
 Gert. Could I believe that temporal goods possessed
My heart, I would myself apply the brand.
 Stauff. Thou art humane, and yet devouring war
Spares not the infant in its mother's arms.
 Gert. From heaven a Friend looks down on innocence:
Direct thy gaze before thee, not behind!
 Stauff. We men may perish, fighting to the last,
But thou, my Gertrude, what might be thy fate?

Gert. The weakest, too, may find, perchance, escape ;
A leap from off this bridge, and I am free.
    Stauff. (throwing himself into her arms.) Who such a
        heart may to his bosom press,
He can for hearth and home with pleasure fight ;
No king exists whose warlike hosts he fears."

" William Tell " was received with deeper and more general enthusiasm than any of Schiller's other writings. Germany was passing through one of the darkest periods of her history ; and the light of this great drama seemed to flame across her sky, giving her hope of brighter days. It is not merely, however, a drama of a particular era ; its matter appeals to permanent elements of human nature, and the qualities of its form are independent of the accidents of place and time.

Schiller left several dramatic plans, at one of which, " Warbeck," he often worked ; and after the completion of " William Tell " he hesitated for some time between it and " Demetrius." Of the latter play we possess (in an incomplete form) the first act, and part of the second. Nothing that Schiller wrote is more full of life than the scene in the Polish Diet with which " Demetrius " opens. There is also a finely poetic spirit in the soliloquy in which Marfa, the widow of Czar Ivan, persuades herself that Demetrius is her son, and rejoices in his approach. These were the last lines written by Schiller, and were found after his death in his portfolio.

CHAPTER XIV.

THE END.

It was the habit of Schiller and Goethe to send each other letters of greeting at the opening of each year. On New-Year's Day 1805, Goethe, on glancing at the letter he had written, saw he had dated it, "The Last New Year." He at once tore the sheet, and beginning another, found to his dismay that he could scarcely resist the impulse to write "The Last New Year" again. With all his enlightenment, there was in Goethe, as in most people, a touch of superstition; and he told Frau von Stein that he had a presentiment that in the course of the year either he or Schiller would die.

Schiller had never quite recovered from the effects of his illness in Jena in the summer of 1804. "The colour of his features changed," says his sister-in-law, Caroline von Wolzogen, "becoming of a greyish hue, so that it often alarmed me." In February 1805 he suffered severely from a series of feverish attacks, which in his weak state of health could not but have disastrous consequences. It happened that Goethe was very ill at the same time; and a young man, Heinrich Voss, a

son of the well-known writer, watched sometimes during
the night with one or other of the poets, both of whom
liked him. He records that Goethe was a rather impatient sufferer, while Schiller was "gentleness itself."
Schiller would not willingly admit his weakness, and
tried hard to soften his wife's distress. On one occasion, about midnight, when she and Voss were with
him, he begged her not to remain longer. As she hesitated, he repeated the request earnestly, and then
almost with passion. She had hardly left the room
when he fainted; and on recovering he was consoled
by remembering that he had been able to send her
away in time. When he became a little better, his
delight, Voss says, was almost childlike; and nothing
pleased him so much as to have his children beside
him, especially his youngest daughter, Emilie, at whom
he would sometimes gaze for a long time, "as if he
wished to think out to the end his infinite happiness in
the possession of such a child." In these last months,
according to Caroline von Wolzogen, "an unspeakable
mildness penetrated his whole being, and revealed itself
in all his thought and feeling: he enjoyed a truly divine
peace." New capacities of appreciation seemed to unfold themselves. Herder's 'Philosophy of the History
of Humanity' had never been quite to his taste; but
"now," he said to Caroline,—"I know not how it is,—
this book speaks to me in an entirely new way, and has
become very dear to me." Music, which did not formerly give him much enjoyment, he began to love; and
on hearing an air by Zingarelli from "Romeo and
Juliet" well sung, he was deeply moved. "Never,"
he declared, "has a song overpowered me in this way."

His calm and hopeful spirit revealed itself in his manner of talking about all subjects, serious and unimportant. "Death," he said, in conversation with his sister-in-law, "cannot be an evil, since it is universal."

When he had sufficiently recovered to visit Goethe, he sent Voss to announce his coming, in case Goethe should not be strong enough to see him. "They fell on each other's necks," says Voss, "and kissed one another, before speaking a word. Neither mentioned his own illness, or that of the other; both gave themselves up to the unmixed pleasure of meeting again with a cheerful spirit." Schiller seized the opportunity of a temporary relief from pain to work at "Demetrius;" and to these days belong some of his most beautiful letters. "For our relation to each other," he wrote to Wilhelm von Humboldt in Rome, "time and space do not exist. Your activity cannot so distract you, and mine cannot so limit and narrow me, as to prevent us from always meeting each other in what is right and worthy. And after all, we are both idealists, and should be ashamed to have it said of us that we did not form things, but that things formed us." To his sister Louise he wrote a kind letter, regretting that their correspondence had been so long interrupted, but expressing his resolve "to take up the thread, and not again to let it be broken." Many plans of travel he formed; and once, talking of a possible trip to the Mediterranean, he suddenly broke out: "I believe I shall be in China yet some day; it would be difficult, no doubt; but I should be unhappy if I were absolutely deprived of the hope."

All these bright visions were to vanish quickly. On the 29th of April, Goethe, although ill, called for him just as Schiller was about to start for the theatre. Goethe could not accompany him, and would not allow him to give up the play; and so they parted at Schiller's door, not again to see each other. Schiller returned from the theatre in high fever; and next day when Voss, who had taken him home, returned, he found Schiller, half asleep, on the sofa. "Here I lie again," he said in a hollow tone. For some days he was fully conscious, and did not seem to suspect that he was in danger. On the evening of the 6th of May he was delirious; but there were occasional flashes of the old spirit. A sheet of Kotzebue's periodical, the 'Freimüthige,' happened to have been brought into his room. "Take it away," he cried, "so that I may say with truth I have not seen it: give me fairy tales and stories of chivalry; in them is the stuff for everything beautiful and great." On the 8th, his sister-in-law having asked how he was, "Ever better, ever more cheerful!" he replied. In the evening of the same day, when the sky was glowing in the sunset, he begged that the curtains of the window might be drawn back: he wished to see the sun. He gazed ardently at the spectacle which he had loved so well; and nature smiled gently on the dying poet. During the night his servant heard him pray to be delivered from a lingering death; and once he roused himself to recite a passage from "Demetrius." Next day (the 9th of May 1805), he was for the most part unconscious; but in the afternoon, as his wife bent over him to smooth his pillow, there was a last kind glance of recognition. She went to tell her sister of this good sign; but both were soon summoned to the sick-room. Lotte knelt by his bed

and pressed his hand, while Caroline, standing beside
the doctor, laid warm cushions on his icy feet. Suddenly an electric shock seemed to flash across his features. His head sank back, and the expression of suffering was transformed into the repose of one who had
quietly fallen asleep.

END OF SCHILLER.